Abbie chuckled as she leaned against the door, her arms crossed firmly against her chest.

'Oh, right, and if I talk what are you going to do? Hit me with that high-wattage charm that works for you so well? I hate to tell you, Romeo, but it won't ever work on me.'

'And what makes you so sure?'

She tilted her chin, the action all defiance. 'I've been charmed by experts and I'm awake to every trick in the book.'

'But you don't know all my tricks.'

A pulse quivered against the pale skin of her throat, completely undoing him, and with a groan Leo gave in and lowered his mouth to hers.

Always an avid reader, **Fiona Lowe** decided to combine her love of romance with her interest in all things medical, so writing Mills & Boon® Medical™ Romance was an obvious choice! She lives in a seaside town in southern Australia, where she juggles writing, reading, working and raising two gorgeous sons, with the support of her own real-life hero! You can visit Fiona's website at www.fionalowe.com

Recent titles by the same author:

THE SURGEON'S SPECIAL DELIVERY
THE DOCTOR CLAIMS HIS BRIDE
THE PLAYBOY DOCTOR'S MARRIAGE
  PROPOSAL

First published in Great Britain 2010
Large Print edition 2011
Harlequin Mills & Boon Limited,
Eton House, 18-24 Paradise Road,
Richmond, Surrey TW9 1SR

© Fiona Lowe 2010

ISBN: 978 0 263 21712 4

Harlequin Mills & Boon policy is to use papers that are
natural, renewable and recyclable products and made
from wood grown in sustainable forests. The logging and
manufacturing process conform to the legal environmental
regulations of the country of origin.

Printed and bound in Great Britain
by CPI Antony Rowe, Chippenham, Wiltshire

HER BROODING ITALIAN SURGEON

BY
FIONA LOWE

HER BROODING ITALIAN SURGEON

In memory of Chris, a caring neighbour
who took great pleasure in sponge cakes,
Mr. Lincoln Roses and thoroughly enjoyed
reading Mills and Boon® Romance.
She'd always cross the road to tell me,
'It's your best one yet, dear.'
Vale, Chris.

Special thanks to Josie and Serena
for their advice on all things Italian.

CHAPTER ONE

BRIGHT white lights radiated heat and sweat poured down Dr Abbie McFarlane's forehead as she gritted her teeth in concentration. A stray strand of hair escaped from her cap but she resisted the urge to wipe her forehead on her sleeve, the sterile law of the operating theatre drilled into her long and hard over many years. Her mouth framed the word 'sponge' but she quickly swallowed it, stealing it back before it tripped over her lips.

Squinting, she tried again. Her nimble hands, which usually deftly and ably sewed fine stitches, seemed at a loss as they plunged yet again down into the sticky mass and stalled.

'*Dottore*, do not stab it. *Il pane*, he needs you to be more gentle.'

Abbie sighed. 'Maria, the dough's just sticking to my fingers and I can't do anything with it.'

'You must use plenty of flour.' Maria's old, gnarled hands quickly scattered more flour on the workbench and expertly kneaded Abbie's sticky mess into a stretchy and elastic dough, before pulling it into a ciabatta roll.

Abbie immediately covered it with a fresh white tea towel. 'I think I'm a lost cause.'

The old woman grinned and shook her scarf-covered head. 'I do this for seventy years. You come again and try.'

Abbie played her only bargaining card in this unusual doctor-patient scenario. 'Only if you promise me you'll rest. Your blood pressure's a bit high and your family's worried about you. It's going to take the new medication a few days to start working, so you have to take it easy.'

'Pfft. I feel fine.' She patted her chest with her fist. 'My heart is strong.'

Abbie frowned and injected a stern tone into her voice. 'If you don't rest I'll put you in hospital.'

Maria sat down fast. 'You sound like my grandson.'

'He must be a wise man, then,' Abbie quipped as she washed her hands in preparation to head back to the clinic.

The eighty-year-old *nonna* rolled her eyes and jabbed the air with her finger. 'He is alone like you.'

'Well, I hope he's as happy as I am.' Abbie

smiled and quickly laid the hand towel over the rail. Twelve months in Bandarra and she'd quickly learned every diversion tactic in the book to avoid being introduced to all and sundry's brothers, sons, cousins and grandsons. She'd even let the 'gay' rumour run wild until one patient had tried to set her up on a date with her daughter. Ironically, no one had made the connection to one of the reasons why she donated so much of her time to the women's shelter—it was the one place no one tried to match her up with anyone. If life had taught her anything, it was that she chose the wrong man every time so staying single was the safe choice. Nothing or no one was going to change that. Ever.

Abbie picked up the keys to her four-wheel drive. 'So, you're going to lie down for an hour until your daughter's back from the vineyard?'

Maria unexpectedly capitulated. 'Yes, *dottore*, I will do as you say.'

'Excellent. I'll call by tomorrow.'

'And I show you how to make bruschetta.'

Abbie laughed. 'Give up now, Maria. I can't cook.'

But the old woman just smiled.

* * *

'Karen, *cara*, my angel of the operating theatre, you can't be serious?' Leo Costa held his overwhelming frustration in check by a bare millimetre, knowing that yelling would work once but flattery worked for ever. Ignoring the pinching of his mobile phone against his ear, he poured on the charm. 'We organised this last week over lunch. I even filled in the paperwork as a special favour to you, so don't break my heart and tell me it's double-booked and I can't have the slot.'

A tiny silence ensued before Karen spoke. 'I guess I could ask Mr Trewellan to reschedule, seeing that we gave him an extra slot last week.'

'I like the way you're thinking, *cara*. Call me back as soon as it's sorted.' He snapped his phone shut without waiting for the theatre administrator's farewell and checked his watch. Damn it, but he was late for rounds and he hated starting the day on the back foot, especially when he had a full appointment list this morning in his Collins Street rooms.

He strode towards the bank of lifts and hit the up button, tapping his foot on the polished linoleum floor of Melbourne City Hospital. He'd had scant sleep last night, having operated on a road trauma case, and it hardly seemed any time at all since he'd left the hospital, and now he was back again. There'd only been enough time to catch a three-hour nap before a quick shower and shave and a much needed shot of espresso before arriving back at work.

As the light above the lift glowed red and the heralding 'ping' sounded, his phone vibrated in his pocket. Hopefully, it was good news about the theatre mess. He flicked his phone open. 'Leo Costa.'

'Oh, thank God, you're not scrubbed.' The unexpected but familiar voice of one of his many sisters came down the line.

'Anna?' He rubbed his hand through his hair. Usually at this time of morning she was knee-deep in children, the school run and juggling calls from restaurant suppliers. 'What's up?'

A half sigh, half cry came down the line. 'It's Nonna, Leo. This time you *have* to come back to Bandarra.'

Abbie stifled a yawn as she swung her red dust-covered boots from her four-by-four onto the hospital car park's sticky asphalt. The hot summer sun had finally fallen below the horizon and

Venus twinkled at her as if to say, *Isn't life wonderful.* But she didn't feel twinkly today. The day had thrown everything at her, including an emergency evacuation from the Aboriginal settlement a hundred kilometres away. Now she longed to crawl out of the clothes she'd been wearing for seventeen hours, ached for a shower to wash the ingrained grit of the outback dust from her skin, and wanted nothing more than to snuggle into soft cotton sheets.

The automatic hospital doors opened and she walked into air-conditioned cool, a blissful respite from the outside summer heat that not even nightfall could cool. She paused, her ears and eyes alert, and then she smiled, letting out a long, slow breath. Calm.

Tonight, the small hospital had the air of quiet, drama-free purpose which, given her day, was exactly what she needed. She'd do a quick check on Maria, consult with the nursing staff about her other two inpatients and then head home and somehow convince Murphy, her Border collie, that he didn't want a walk tonight.

The nursing station was empty, but the charts had been gathered for the ease of the night shift and sorted into alphabetical order. She quickly rifled through them until she found the group labelled 'Rossi'.

'Page her doctor again.' A rich baritone voice, threaded with startling steel, travelled down the corridor, followed a beat later by, 'I'd really appreciate it, Erin.' The steel in the voice had vanished, replaced by a deep mellow sound reminiscent of a luxurious velvet cloak that wrapped enticingly around a person and caressed with beguiling softness.

Abbie knew all about velvet hiding steel. She'd grown up with it in many guises and it had chased her through a disastrous relationship. Charm so often hid threatening control.

'Of course, Mr Costa, I'll try again for you.' Erin Bryant, the immensely capable no-nonsense night-duty nurse who always did things her way, had just been vanquished with Charm 101. The fact that a relative was even in the hospital at this time of night was testament to that.

Holding the multicoloured charts, Abbie grinned, knowing that for the first time today the fates had actually come down on her side. She didn't have a Costa in hospital and Justin, her most recent locum who'd been gleefully counting down the days until he left for his cross-Asia trek back to his home town of London, would have to deal with this determined relative as one of his last obligations. Being British, he did polite much better than she did. Humming to herself, she walked down the corridor to Maria's room, turned into the doorway and stopped dead.

A man stood just inside the door, his presence filling the room with vibrating energy that swirled and eddied like a tornado, pulling at everything and everyone in its path.

An involuntary shiver shot through Abbie, immediately chased by a foreign flicker of heat. Heat that hadn't glowed in a very long time.

No way, not possible. But her hand instinctively tightened around the charts.

Erin's face beamed with a high-wattage smile. 'This is Dr McFarlane, Mr Costa, and I'll go and get you that coffee I promised.' Still smiling, she backed towards the door.

'*Grazie*, Erin.' His head tilted and his lips curved into a smile that travelled along black-stubble cheeks, and for a fraction of a second it lit up his eyes like the bright-white light of Venus.

Abbie took in a deep breath just as Maria's unknown visitor turned his unrelenting gaze to her.

A gaze that shot from eyes as black as the night sky but was now minus the twinkle. One bold dark brow lifted as he took in her dust-streaked shorts, her crumpled and stained polo shirt and her uncontrollable mass of chaotic curls. Judging by the expression in the depths of his onyx eyes, he found everything about her eminently lacking.

Abbie needed to lift her chin to meet his scrutiny and if he, a patient's relative, had the temerity to openly give her the once-over, then *right back at you, pal*. But that was when irony socked her hard like a sucker-punch to the gut.

A strong, straight nose centred his Roman face and high cheekbones defined it as striking, but it was his well-shaped lips that told the truth— gorgeous and well aware of it. Despite the fatigue that played around his eyes and hovered near a jagged white scar on his square jaw, the man could have modelled for fashion week, although she sensed he'd have taken no nonsense and would have probably given the organisers a very hard time.

He was urban chic from his glossy indigo hair down to his Italian leather loafers. A black V-necked light cotton sweater clung to, and curved around, broad square shoulders, toned pecs and a flat stomach, boldly advertising the buff goods that nestled below. Soft and cool dune-coloured linen trousers caressed long, long legs unsullied by any hint of outback red earth or heat-induced perspiration. If she wasn't standing in front of him breathing in his scent of mint mixed with orange, she would have dismissed him as a mythical being that no mere mortal could ever hope to emulate.

She dropped her gaze and frantically gathered her scattered thoughts, focusing on the fact that she was the doctor and he was her patient's relative. She was therefore the one in charge. Dealing with relatives was something she prided herself on. She understood their occasional outbursts as a projection of fear and feelings of powerlessness in a foreign environment and, after all, hospitals were strange and frightening places for the general public. But absolutely nothing about this man looked uncertain or unsure, or powerless.

His firm stance of controlled casualness rippled with panther-like readiness and he spoke before Abbie could introduce herself. 'You're Nonna's doctor?' Incredulity mixed with a hint of censure rode on the words.

A shaft of determination straightened her spine.

So what that she was dirty and grimy and he was 'Mr Ultra-Clean and well-kempt from the city'; he hadn't just spent the afternoon in the middle of nowhere keeping a young boy alive until the Flying Doctors had arrived. Given those neatly trimmed, dirt-free nails, he was probably an accountant and the closest he got to life and death was a wobbly row of figures.

It was hard to peer imperiously down her nose when he towered over her five foot two inches, so instead she extended her hand with crisp efficiency. 'Abbie McFarlane, GP, and you would be?'

He suddenly smiled, dimples spiralling into the inky stubble as his hand gripped hers. 'Leo Costa, Maria's grandson.'

Unambiguous sexual electricity zapped her so hard she saw stars. She pulled her hand back fast and somehow managed a garbled, 'Oh, right, yes, she mentioned you when I saw her yesterday', while trying to rein her wanton body back under the tight control she'd held it in for three years. Not an easy task after being broadsided by the explosive combination of his touch and smile. A smile that should come complete with a classification warning.

She caught a glance of the sleeping Maria, which immediately centred her, and she instinctively stepped back out into the corridor. 'Let's not wake your grandmother.'

Like a giant cat, Leo Costa moved forward with rippling fluidity, stepping into the space she'd just vacated, his energy ramming into her, setting up more unwanted and inappropriate tingling.

'How long have you been my grandmother's doctor?' The casual question, asked in a conversational tone, was at odds with the tension hovering across his shoulders and narrowing his eyes.

She thought about how long she'd actually known Maria and the time it had taken to convince her to accept an examination. 'A few weeks—'

'And you saw her yesterday?' The conversational tone slipped slightly.

Abbie nodded. 'I did. She was trying to teach me how to bake bread but—'

'A sick woman was teaching you to bake bread at a time when you should have been admitting her to hospital.'

His words were a shot across the bow, in stark

contrast to the captivating smile. Warning bells rang loud in her head. 'I beg your pardon?'

He spoke quietly but every word reverberated like the strike against a bell. 'If you'd admitted my grandmother to hospital yesterday and monitored her more closely, she wouldn't have had a stroke.'

She sucked in a breath, hearing it whistle between her teeth. *Stay calm.* 'Mr Costa, I understand you're upset, as am I. Your grandmother is a very special woman but she didn't have malignant hypertension, which is extremely high blood pressure. Although her blood pressure was elevated, based on her observations yesterday, there was no need to admit her.'

He casually crossed his arms over his chest but she caught a silver flash of steel in his black eyes. 'You prescribed medication?'

She pursed her lips. 'Yes, she was commenced on medication to lower her blood pressure and she was instructed to rest.'

The corner of his mouth seemed at war with the twitching muscle in his jaw but the attempted smile lost out and the charm he'd used with Erin, and half-tried with her, totally vanished. 'And I put it to you that the medication was too strong and brought her BP down too fast, causing a focal cerebral ischemia.'

Focal cerebral ischemia? O-K. Maria's grandson definitely wasn't an accountant. His commanding control of the room suddenly made sense, although it struck her as odd that Maria hadn't mentioned her grandson was a doctor. That aside, his grandmother was *her* patient, not his and Maria's medical care had been textbook.

'Mr Costa—' she emphasised his title '—I'm assuming your expertise is in a branch of surgery not geriatrics.'

Dark eyes flashed before a tight smile stretched his mouth. 'I'm a trauma surgeon at Melbourne City with a private practice of general surgery. I don't believe you're a geriatrician either.'

Touché. The bald statement carried power and credence and told of a man used to getting his own way. She had a pretty good idea how he usually got what he wanted—with effortless charm and good looks—and, if that failed, he used a bulldozer.

Well, she wasn't about to be bulldozed. Not this time.

'Your grandmother hasn't seen a doctor in over two years and it took me a few weeks to convince her to let me examine her. I diagnosed her hypertension a few days ago. Although there's a slight chance that perhaps the medication lowered her blood pressure too quickly, it's far more probable that the stroke was caused by longstanding hypertension. She has a slight weakness on her right side but I'm very confident that with rehabilitation and time, it will resolve.'

'I'm glad you're confident.'

The disapproval in the quietly spoken words plunged deep like the cut of cold steel. She matched his black gaze. 'I'm very confident.'

He shrugged his broad shoulders and stared down at her, his eyes filled with condescension and backlit with righteous resolve. 'Look, I'm sure you've done *your* best but I know you'll understand when I say I want my *nonna*'s care transferred to another doctor.'

I know you'll understand. Outrage poured through Abbie and she clenched her hands by her sides to stop herself from lunging at his gorgeous but arrogant throat. Greg had used the very same words. So had her father just before he'd left. Somehow through clenched teeth she managed to speak. 'That's surely up to Maria.'

His head moved almost imperceptibly, the light

catching his hair, the sheen so bright it dazzled. 'Nonna usually takes my advice.'

It was a statement of fact spoken by a successful man. A man raised in the heart of a loving Italian family where education and experience were honoured and family was everything. The polar opposite of her own family.

She'd been left with no doubt that Leo Costa would advise his grandmother against her and she knew she had scant chance against the power of his recommendation, no matter how wrong she believed it to be. He had both the money and contacts to pull strings. 'Perhaps she might surprise you.'

Unfathomable dark eyes stared at her. 'I doubt that.'

Abbie forced herself to smile and to behave in the proper way a doctor should—putting her patient's needs first, irrespective of her own feelings. 'As Maria's asleep and her health and welfare are my paramount concerns, the decision will rest until morning.' She extended her arm towards the exit with an in-charge sweep. 'Good night, Mr Costa.'

He gave her a slight nod of acquiescence along with a wry smile, as if he'd just glimpsed something completely unexpected. 'Until the morning then, Abbie.'

He turned on his heel and somehow she forced her wobbly legs to hold her up until the doors opened and he was swallowed up by the night. She sank against the wall, hating the butterflies in her stomach that floated on a current of heat, trailing through her and upending every resolution she'd made three years ago.

Leo Costa with his effortless charm, devastating good looks and single-minded purpose was her worst nightmare and she was determined not to relive bad dreams. She gulped in air and her tattered resolve slowly wove itself back together. Warrior Abbie stood firm and spoke sternly. *You'll miss Maria but you don't need him anywhere near you.*

And she couldn't argue with that.

CHAPTER TWO

'HAVE you lost your mind?' Anna slid a hot and frothy breakfast cappuccino towards Leo across the large wooden kitchen table.

'It was an unwise thing for you to do.' Rosa, his mother, quietly rebuked him as she passed a plate of fluffy light pastries and pushed two onto his plate.

Leo clung to his temper by a thread. Coming back to Bandarra always set him on edge but if he just breathed slowly, let them have their say, then he could move forward with the day doing things his way. He'd organise Nonna's care and then catch the afternoon flight back to the sanctuary of Melbourne. Breaking open the brioche, he slathered it with home-made raspberry jam, the sweet breakfast in stark contrast to the muesli he always ate in his Melbourne apartment. But the kitchen in Bandarra was a world away from Melbourne, despite the fact there was only a six-hundred-kilometre distance between the two places.

Rosa carefully stirred sugar into her coffee. 'I wish you'd come home rather than going direct from the airport to the hospital, and then all this could have been avoided.'

For the second time in twenty-four hours his usual sanguine approach slipped and his voice rose sharply. 'This is Nonna we're talking about! Of course I went straight to the hospital, especially as I'd had both you and Anna sobbing on the phone, not to mention Bianca and Chiara's texts.'

His gut clenched as a ripple of fear spread its dread again, just as it had last night when he'd stood at the end of the narrow hospital bed watching his amazing Nonna, always such a powerhouse of energy, looking so frail and tiny under crisp white sheets. He hated that feeling, that powerlessness and the way it dragged him back into the past. Back to the waterhole, back to failing Dom so badly. He abruptly rubbed his chin. 'I wasn't leaving until I'd spoken with her doctor, which is what I thought you wanted.'

His mother threw him a rueful smile. 'Considering how stubborn Nonna can be, Abbie

McFarlane's been a saint. I told her how worried I was about your grandmother and she put up with all of Nonna's tricks and made home visits until Nonna finally let her examine her.'

Anna laughed. 'True, but not even Nonna has been able to teach Abbie to cook—she's hopeless.'

Leo frowned against the recurring and un-wanted image of tangled and tumbling cinnamon-sprinkled caramel curls framing rainforest-green eyes. Eyes that hadn't flickered with the keen appreciation he was used to seeing when he met women's gazes. The vision had interrupted his sleep and increased his irritation. Women like Abbie McFarlane never got picked up by his radar, let alone landed a starring role in his dreams. With the exception of his ill-conceived marriage, where he'd been faithful to Christina, he'd always had his pick of women, and all his choices came with statuesque height, haute couture and heavenly features.

Name one that has really interested you in the last year.

Not wanting to go there, he pulled his mind back to the conversation. 'Well, I don't care about her cooking, or the fact she doesn't even look like a doctor. *I* wasn't impressed by her medicine.'

Anna raised both of her neatly shaped brows, taking in his crisp outfit of navy knee-length shorts teamed with a short-sleeved chambray shirt. 'Big brother, you've turned into a big city fashion snob. Abbie might dress like a female version of a crocodile hunter but her medicine's spot on. She's done more for this community in twelve months than old Doctor Renton did in his twelve years.'

Annoyance fizzed in his veins. 'That isn't saying much then, is it?'

His father, Stefano, who'd been silent behind the most recent edition of *Vintners' Monthly*, lowered the magazine. Wise molasses-coloured eyes stared back at Leo from behind rimless lenses. 'Your mistake is you've forgotten Bandarra isn't Melbourne and the choice of doctors here is seriously limited.'

Rosa sighed. 'Your *nonna*'s getting old, *figlio mio.*'

No. He wanted to put his hands over his ears like he'd done as a little child when he didn't want to hear. Right now he didn't want to hear or think about Nonna and death. Nonna was such a special part of his life. She featured in every childhood memory—always there giving hugs while his parents had been busy establishing the vineyard, clipping him around the ear when he got too cheeky and always feeding him like he was a king.

Holding him so tightly after the accident.

Right then his exasperation with his family peaked. Enough! He'd let everyone have their say and now it was his turn. 'I'm the qualified medical practitioner in this conversation and I've made a decision which I intend to follow through on.' He pushed back his chair, the red-gum scraping loud against the polished boards.

'You go and be the doctor but Nonna doesn't just need that.' Stefano rose to his feet and his quiet but determined voice stalled Leo's departure. 'Most of all she needs you to be a grandson and to give of your time. In fact, all of your family needs your time.'

Leo's throat tightened and every part of him tensed, all primed and ready to flee. For years he'd flown in and flown out of Bandarra, only ever staying forty-eight hours, often less. 'Papà, I can't. Work is busy.'

'Work is always busy.' His father downed the

last of his coffee. 'You managed to arrange things so you could be here for Nonna. I'm certain you can arrange to stay longer if you choose. You haven't been home for a vintage since you were eighteen and we've never asked you to come, but you're here now. This time you need to stay for Nonna, your mother and the rest of us.' His hand settled on Rosa's shoulder and he gave her a gentle squeeze.

Leo's breath stuck in his chest as he tried to think of a way out, a way to avoid having to stay. Excuses rose to his lips but his father's implacable stance and knowing expression silenced them. His father would see them for what they were— excuses. The ties of family tightened around him, pulling him back to a place he didn't want to be.

Anna winked at him. 'Come on, big brother, stay a while. It'll be just like the old days, lots of fun.'

But fun was the last thing a holiday in Bandarra could ever be.

Bubbling frustration tinged with fury ate at Leo as he shifted in the car seat, unable to get comfortable. Bandarra Car Rentals didn't run to a

Ferrari Spider and he was stuck in a small car which wasn't designed for men who were five foot six, let alone six foot one.

Although not even nine a.m., heat poured through the untinted windows, declaring that the day would be a scorcher. He pulled on his aviator sunglasses and slammed down the visor. His father hadn't pulled rank like that in seventeen years. On top of that, he couldn't get over his family's attitude towards Nonna's medical care. Didn't they want the best for her?

Perhaps she already has the best with Abbie McFarlane.

No, he couldn't believe that. The woman had disaster written all over her, from the rent in her khaki trousers to the burnt-red ochre smear on her freckle-dusted cheeks. Smooth, soft cheeks. He shook away the image and focused on his concerns. She looked about twenty-one, although he knew she had to be older than that, but still, she had the chaotic look of someone who could hardly look after herself, let alone patients. Nonna needed someone with solid experience—years and years of experience. Not someone with the bare basics of a couple of intern years, who still held a textbook in one hand and a prayer in the other.

It was well known that the further a person lived from a major capital city the more their health was compromised by their lack of access to state-of-the-art health care. That was a given in Bandarra, but at least it still had a small hospital which meant it attracted more doctors than other outback towns. He intended to talk to the senior practice partner—that was the doctor who should be looking after Nonna, not the trainee GP.

Vineyards and orchards flashed past as he headed into town, the rich red loamy river soil contrasting intensely with the grape-green foliage of the 'close-to-harvest' vines. The familiar clutch of unease tightened another notch and his chest hurt the way it always did when he found himself back under Bandarra's endless outback sky. His fingers whitened as he gripped the steering wheel overly hard and he concentrated on forcing away the demons that threatened to suffocate him. Pulling hard left, he deliberately avoided the river road, taking a longer route, a route that he could navigate with his eyes closed despite the fact he'd lived in Melbourne a very long time. Avoiding the river was the only way he was going to survive three to four weeks in Bandarra.

Visitors to the district were always amazed at how the pioneers had harnessed the power of the great Murray River and turned what should have been an arid and harsh land into the luxuriant and premier fruit basket of Australia. But back then the river had run with a lot more water and the current irrigators now faced a new set of problems that the pioneers had probably never envisaged.

Ten minutes later, Leo walked into the hospital and caught sight of the broad back of a male standing at the nurses' station. He was wearing a white coat. Leo smiled—now that was more like it.

'Excuse me.'

The doctor raised his head from the chart and turned his shirt-and-tie-covered torso towards him. 'May I help you?'

The English accent surprised Leo but this doctor had a gravitas that Abbie McFarlane lacked, despite the *Star Trek* tie. He extended his hand. 'Leo Costa, surgeon. Are you the Senior Medical Officer?'

'No, but I'd be happy to introduce you.' He shot out his hand. 'Justin Willoughby. It's brilliant that you're going to be working here.'

'*No!*' Hell would freeze over before he'd work in Bandarra.

Justin started with surprise at his emphatic tone and Leo sucked in a calming breath. In Melbourne he was known for high standards but with an easy-going approach. He wouldn't let a short time in Bandarra steal that from him. 'Sorry, what I meant to say is, I'm Maria Rossi's grandson and I'm just up here for a few weeks until things are sorted out with my grandmother. Then it's *straight* back to Melbourne.'

'Ah.' Justin nodded but his expression remained disappointed. 'Pity. Bandarra could do with a visiting surgeon. The SMO's caught up in ED. This way.' He inclined his head and started walking down the corridor.

Leo fell into step with Justin and followed him through double perspex doors into a compact emergency department. Screens were drawn around cubicles and a pretty nurse walked towards them.

'Where's the boss, Lisa?' Justin asked.

'Not far away.'

'Leo, you stay here and I'll bring the boss to you. Back in a mo.'

Justin disappeared, leaving Leo with the nurse,

who gave him a none too subtle look of curiosity which finished with smouldering interest. 'Hello. New to Bandarra?'

'I grew up here.' The words came out stark and brusque and he immediately forced himself to return her friendly look with a flash of his trademark smile. A smile he used many times a day without even thinking because it was never wise to burn bridges. His smile had gained him all sorts of things and had got him out of a few nasty situations. *Except for yesterday.*

Yesterday had been an aberration. His cool had slipped slightly with Abbie McFarlane and he'd chalked it up to his shock about Nonna and being back in a town he tried very hard to avoid. But everyone made mistakes and thankfully no real harm had been done.

'Were you a blockie?' Lisa used the local term to describe people who grew fruit on land with irrigation rights.

'My grandfather was.'

'Oh, are you related to the Italians out by Wadjera billabong?'

The name plunged into Leo like a knife to the heart and he stiffened. Thankfully, Justin's return ended the conversation.

'Leo, I'd like to introduce you to our SMO.'

Leo turned with a welcoming smile on his face. A pair of questioning moss-green eyes hit him with a clear and uncompromising gaze. Eyes that slanted seductively at the corners. A burst of unexpected heat fired low in his belly, disconcerting him for a second before reality crashed in, wiping out all other feeling. *Our SMO.* Damn it, how could she possibly be the senior doctor?

You've forgotten Bandarra isn't Melbourne. His father's voice rang loud in his head and the full ramifications of what he'd done last night hit him like a king punch. He'd let the Bandarra demons get to him and had made an ill-judged call.

He pulled himself together and, with aching cheeks, smiled. 'Abbie.'

Her mouth flattened. 'Leo.'

A startled expression crossed Justin's face. 'So you two have met before?'

'We met last night.' Abbie tugged at the edges of a clean starched white coat which covered a plain round-neck T-shirt and a straight no-frills navy skirt. The hiking boots had been replaced by flat utilitarian sandals of nondescript brown.

Not a trace of make-up touched her face but, despite that, her lips had a luminous sheen that pulled Leo's gaze and held it fast. What the hell was wrong with him? But he didn't have time to second-guess his reaction—the moment had come for damage control. He forced a self-deprecating quirk to his lips and gave a European shrug of his shoulders. 'I didn't realise Abbie was the SMO. A major error on my part.'

Justin laughed, giving his boss a cheeky grin. 'Poor Abs, if you were a bloke you could grow a beard to look older.' He winked at Leo. 'She might forgive you in time.'

Going by the implacable set of her face and the tight pull of skin over her cheekbones, Leo wasn't so sure. Still, that didn't matter because he'd pull in a favour and ask the doctor from Naroopna to take over. 'May we speak in private?'

She matched his shrug and rolled her hands palm up. 'Is there anything left to say? You made your position quite clear last night.' Turning on her heel, she headed towards the perspex doors and thumped them open.

Ignoring the intrigued looks of the other staff, he walked with her. 'I do have something to say.'

'You surprise me.' Her sarcasm radiated from her like heat haze. She unexpectedly turned left into an empty ward and then spun back, crossing her arms hard against her chest, pushing her breasts upward. 'Look, Leo, I don't have time for this; I have patients waiting. Are you flying in a private doctor or transferring Maria to Mildura or Melbourne?'

He found it hard to resist sneaking a look at her surprising cleavage. 'Neither one of those options is my choice.' No matter how persuasive he knew he could be, there was no way he'd be able to convince Nonna to leave Bandarra. She'd lived here since arriving as a bride from Italy back in the fifties. Perhaps there'd been times in the past when she might have toyed with the idea of leaving but, since the accident, she'd refused even visits to Melbourne. She wouldn't leave Dominico. Leo alone had been the one to run.

He rubbed his chin and hauled his thoughts back to the here and now. 'You can hand over her care to David Martin.'

A deep V formed at the bridge of her nose. 'So you're transferring her to Adelaide?'

What? 'No, she's staying here.' He tilted his head slightly and met her gaze. 'Abbie.' He paused for the briefest moment, the beat lending credence to his upcoming words. 'Thank you for your care.

This isn't personal; it's just that David's experience is what Nonna needs.'

For the first time since he'd met her, a smile pulled her generous mouth upwards. It danced along her cheeks and into her eyes, making them sparkle like the rainforest after rain. And then she laughed. A laugh tinged with incredulity and yet grounded with a known truth, as if she'd heard a similar story before. As if she saw straight through him.

A flicker of unease stirred his normally unshakeable confidence.

'It's been a while since you last visited Bandarra, hasn't it?'

And, just like that, he felt the power shift. 'What makes you say that?'

'David Martin moved to Adelaide ten months ago and the practice at Naroopna is vacant. As is the one at Budjerree. Right now, Bandarra is the only township within two hundred kilometres with medical staff. Come Wednesday, when Justin leaves, it's just me and the nursing staff.'

His breakfast turned to stone in his gut. All he'd wanted was the best for Nonna. Instead, he'd let fatigue and fear of the past interfere with his usual clear-thinking and now he'd backed himself into a corner.

The urgent bleep of her pager suddenly blared between them and she checked the liquid display. Without a word, she sprinted past him and out of the room, leaving behind only a lingering and delectable scent of strawberries and liquorice.

He hated that he instinctively took in a deeper breath.

Abbie raced into a chaotic ED, shedding all of her disconcerting and unsuitable thoughts about the infuriating and ridiculously gorgeous Leo Costa. There should be a law against men being that handsome, and a statute that stopped her even noticing. The piercing siren of an ambulance screamed in the distance, instantly focusing her with its howling volume that increased with every moment. An intense sound that never brought good news.

People were everywhere. Two teenagers sat pale and silent holding each other's hands, an elderly man supported a woman to a chair and a young woman clutching a baby called out, 'Help me,' and still people poured through the doors, many bloodied and hurt.

Lisa and Jason were murmuring platitudes mixed in with firm instructions as they tried to examine a hysterical woman with blood streaming down her face. Her shrieks of anguish bounced off the walls, telling a story of terror and pain.

The area looked like a war zone. 'What's happened and why haven't emergency services notified us?'

Justin grimaced. 'Apparently a bus hit a truck. Those who could, walked here.'

Triage. Years of training swung into action. 'Lisa, you're on walking wounded. Get a nurse from the floor to help you stat, and get someone to ring all the nursing staff and tell them to come in. I want a list of all names and all injuries. Prioritise, treat and be aware of anyone who blacked out. Any concerns, consult me or Jason.'

'Will do.' The experienced nurse headed to the chairs as Abbie grabbed the emergency radio.

'Bandarra Base Hospital to Bandarra Police, over.'

Daniel Ruston's voice crackled down the line. 'Abbie, a bus and a truck collided. The paramedics are on their way with the first of the seriously injured passengers. It's not pretty.'

'How many are there?'

'Two at least, probably more.'

'Thanks, over and out.' She headed straight into the resuss room, which was technically always set up ready for any emergency but she always liked to double-check. She glanced at the brand-new Virtual Trauma and Critical Care Service—a video conferencing screen on wheels. With its camera that used superfast broadband technology to transfer images from the country to the city, GPs in small towns could teleconference with specialists if need be. It was an extra medical lifeline in the tyranny of distance. Everything was ready. She didn't have to wait long.

The paramedics barrelled through the doors, their stretchers bringing in two patients, both wearing oxygen masks. Paul, the senior paramedic, his face grim, started talking. 'First patient is Jenny, a thirty-year-old woman, conscious with pneumothorax and suspected abdominal internal injuries. Chest tube and IV inserted in the field but BP continuing to drop. Second patient is Emma, a seventeen-year-old female with suspected spinal injuries, currently on spinal board and immobilised with a collar. Complaining of not feeling legs. IV inserted in the field and observations stable.'

Abbie bit her lip. 'What else is coming?'

Paul looked sombre. 'There's a forty-five-year-old male with a fractured pelvis and multiple lacerations, and a sixty-year-old woman whose leg has gone into the wall of the bus. Jaws of life are on hand.'

Adrenaline poured through her, making her shake. She had at least four seriously ill patients, a minimum of thirty walking wounded and only four staff until the other nurses arrived. The ratio of staff to patients totally sucked.

'It hurts.' Jenny's muffled sob came from behind the oxygen mask.

Abbie put her hand reassuringly on the woman's shoulder as the trolley was wheeled into the resuss room. 'I'm Abbie McFarlane and I'll give you something for pain as soon as I've examined you.'

Justin appeared. 'Lisa's got it under control out there and I've given the hysterical woman a sedative and will stitch her forehead later. If you're right here, I'll examine the other stretcher patient.'

'Great. Thanks.' Abbie wrapped the automatic

blood pressure cuff around Jenny's arm and attached the electrodes to the ECG dots that the paramedics had applied. The reassuring beat of a regular heart rate traced across the screen.

The blood pressure machine beeped. Eighty on fifty.

Not good. 'I just have to feel your tummy, Jenny.'

'Will it hurt?' Fear lit the woman's eyes.

'It might.' Abbie gently palpated the woman's abdomen and her fingers met a rigid and guarded upper left quadrant.

Jenny flinched. 'Do you have to do that?'

'I'm sorry.' *She's bleeding somewhere.*

'What do you need? Catheter, plasma expander, abdominal ultrasound?' Erin walked into the room, lack-of-sleep-induced black smudges under her eyes but as competent as ever.

'All of the above, Erin.' *And more.*

Despite what Leo Costa thought of her, Abbie knew her medicine, knew her strengths and was well aware of her shortcomings. She was a bloody good GP but she wasn't a surgeon.

A patient with internal bleeding needed a surgeon.

She glanced hopefully at the Virtual Trauma

and Critical Care Service but knew in her heart that this time a 'virtual' surgeon wasn't going to meet her needs. She needed a real live hands-on surgeon and she had one down the hall.

One who thought she was incompetent. One she wanted to avoid at all costs, not work with side by side. But her breath shuddered out of her lungs, the sound telling. No matter how much she wanted to avoid the charismatic and opinionated Leo Costa, patients' needs and lives came first.

The BP machine screamed incessantly, telling its undeniable message in no uncertain terms. Jenny was bleeding into her abdominal cavity. It was just a matter of time before she had more blood there than in her arteries.

She grabbed the plasma expander and plunged the sharp tip of the IV into it, piercing the seal, and then hung the bag onto the hook, opening the flow to full bore. Her choice was no choice at all. Jenny needed surgery and Abbie had to ask for help.

'Erin, find Leo Costa and get him in here. Now!'

CHAPTER THREE

ABBIE had just finished catheterising Jenny when Leo strode into the room, instantly filling it with vibrating energy and command.

'You want me?'

His onyx eyes held hers with a hypnotic gaze and a sharp pang akin to hunger shook her so hard her fingers almost dropped the forceps. It had been years since she'd experienced anything like it. She cleared her throat, finding her in-charge voice. 'Jenny sustained a blunt trauma to the abdomen, is haemodynamically unstable and transfer to Melbourne at this point is risky. She needs a surgeon.' She pulled the ultrasound machine in close and turned it on, handing the transducer to him as Erin returned with a set of charts.

Leo put his hand gently on the terrified patient's arm and, using the velvet tone she'd heard him use with everyone except herself, he reassured their patient.

'Jenny, I'm Leo Costa and I'm a surgeon. Dr McFarlane's pretty concerned about you so I'm just going to see what's going on using the ultrasound.'

'OK.' Jenny gazed up at Leo as if he'd mesmerised her and all the resistance she'd used with Abbie melted away.

Abbie's jaw clenched as memories of her father and Greg swamped her but she reminded herself it didn't matter a jot if Leo Costa charmed every woman he ever met as long as he saved Jenny in a professional manner.

'It will feel cold.' He squirted the gel onto her abdomen and gently moved it across her distended belly. Black and white flickered on the screen until the image came into focus. He let out a low grunt. 'Good catch.'

Abbie followed the trace of his finger against the screen, making out the black mass that was darker than intact liver and splenic tissue. It was everywhere—between the left kidney and the spleen, behind the spleen and ultimately pooling in the pelvis, the blood having travelled via the paracolic gutter. Her diagnosis was correct, not that it made her feel at all happy because Jenny wasn't out of the woods yet.

Leo wiped the transducer and stowed it in its holder on the machine and returned his undivided attention to the patient. 'Jenny, I'm fairly certain the impact of the accident has ruptured your spleen and I'm going to have to operate.'

The already pale woman blanched even more, a tremble of fear on her lips. 'You're good at this, aren't you?'

Leo grinned, his smile streaking across his clean-shaven cheeks. 'Jenny, I'm more than good; I'm one of the best.' Then, as impossible as it was to imagine, his voice suddenly dropped even deeper, its timbre completely sincere. 'Most importantly for you, I've done this operation many times in Melbourne. Erin's going to get you ready for Theatre and I'll see you there very soon.'

Abbie knew at that moment if she'd been the patient she would have followed him to the ends of the earth. Thank goodness she wasn't. She was a wise and experienced woman and she didn't follow any man anywhere. Not any more.

Leo tilted his head towards the door, code for, *We need to talk*, and then strode towards it. Abbie followed him out into the corridor.

Without preliminaries, he cut to the chase. 'Can you anaesthetise?'

She nodded. 'I can and Erin can assist but that's all the staff I can spare because Justin and the nursing staff are needed down here.'

'Abbie—' Justin hurried towards them '—I'm evacuating the spinal injury to Melbourne by air ambulance.'

'What about the elderly woman?'

'She hasn't arrived yet; they're still trying to get her out but Paul's worried about a crush injury and possible risk of amputation.'

Abbie groaned. 'Man, I wish I could clone us. We've still got the fractured pelvis to assess. Get the paramedics to help you when they bring in the next two patients and—'

'Abbie.' Her name came out on a low growl as Leo slid his arm under her elbow in an attempt to propel her forward. 'We need to get to Theatre now.'

His urgency roared through her, along with a tremor of something else she refused to name. 'Justin if you—'

'He'll ring us in Theatre if he needs to consult. Come on.' Leo marched her back into the resuss room. 'Erin, *cara*, let's move.' He started to push the trolley through the door.

Then he swung back to Abbie, his well-shaped lips twitching with an unexpected smile tinged with cheeky humour as if he'd just realised something funny. 'Er... Abbie, exactly where is the operating theatre?'

Her already adrenaline-induced limbs liquefied. She could resist his *getting my own way* smile, knowing it was manufactured, but this smile was vastly different—it was one hundred per cent genuine and completely devastating. Somehow she forced her boneless legs to start moving. 'This way; follow me.'

'It's a mess in here.' Dealing with the pulped spleen made Leo frown in concentration as he carefully separated it from its anchoring ligaments. Every part of him operated on high-alert, not just because all emergency surgery meant the unknown but because added into this combination was working with today's less experienced staff. Still, he couldn't fault either of them. Abbie McFarlane had run the emergency as well as any of his veteran colleagues in Melbourne and right now she was coping with a tricky anaesthetic and acting as scout.

'Suction please, Erin.' The amount of blood in the field had him extremely worried. 'Abbie, how's her pressure?'

Remarkably calm green eyes peered from behind a surgical mask. 'Holding, but only just. I'll be happier when you've zapped the sucker.'

He grimaced behind his mask. 'You and me both.' He moved the probe into position and, using his foot, activated the diathermy. The zap sounded loud in the relatively quiet theatre, in stark contrast to Melbourne City where his favourite music was always piped in.

Erin's hand hovered, holding the suction over the clean site, and he counted slowly. By the time he got to four, blood bubbled up again, filling the space. 'Damn it.' He packed in more gauze.

'Pressure's still dropping.' A fray in Abbie's calm unravelled in her voice. 'She's lost three litres of blood and this is our last packed cell until the helicopter arrives.'

'It will be OK.' He said it as much for himself as to reassure Abbie and Erin. Closing out the sound of the beeping machines, he carefully examined the entire operation site millimetre by millimetre, looking for the culprit.

'O2 sats are dropping.' Stark urgency rang in Abbie's voice.

The gurgling sound of the suction roared around him as Jenny's life-force squirted into the large bottle under the operating table almost as fast as Abbie could pump it in. A flash of memory suddenly exploded in his head. Him. Raised voices. Christina's screams. Dom. Life ebbing away.

His heart raced and he dragged in a steadying breath. He hadn't known how to save Dom and he'd failed Christina but he was saving this woman.

Look harder. He caught a glimpse of something and immediately fritzed it with the diathermy. Still the blood gurgled back at him. He held out his hand. 'Four-zero.'

'She's about one minute away from arresting.' Abbie hung up the last unit of blood, her forehead creased in anxiety.

'I'm on it.' Sending all his concentration down his fingers, he carefully looped the silk around the bleeding vessel and made a tie. Then he counted.

This time the site stayed miraculously clear.

His chest relaxed, releasing the breath he hadn't been aware he was holding.

'Pressure's rising, O2 sats are rising.' Relief poured through Abbie's voice as she raised her no-nonsense gaze to his. 'You had me worried.'

Despite her words, he caught a fleeting glimpse of approbation in the shimmering depths of green. 'Hey, I'm Italian—we always go for the big dramatic finish.'

Abbie blinked, her long brown lashes touching the top of her mask, and then she laughed. A full-bodied, joyous laugh that rippled through her, lighting up her eyes, dancing across her forehead and jostling the stray curl that had sneaked out from under her unflattering theatre cap.

And you thought she was plain? He frowned at the unwelcome question as he started to close the muscle layers.

Abbie administered pethidine for pain relief through a pump. 'Well, we Anglo-Saxons prefer the quiet life.'

'Speak for yourself. I'm not averse to a bit of drama and flair. It makes life interesting.' Erin fluttered her pretty lashes at him over her surgical mask, an open sign of *if you're interested, then I'm definitely in.*

The day his divorce had been finalised fifteen years ago, he'd committed to dating beautiful women and dating often—a strategy that served him well. He loved women and enjoyed their company—he just didn't want to commit to one woman. The emotional fallout of his marriage had put paid to that. Now he focused on work, saving lives and enjoying himself. It was a good plan because it left him very little time to think about anything else.

Usually when he was given such an open invitation as the attractive Erin had just bestowed, he smiled, called her *cara mia*, took her out to dinner and then spent a fun few weeks before the next pretty nurse caught his eye or he caught the glimpse of marriage and babies in her eyes.

But recently that game had got tired.

The theatre phone rang and Abbie took the call. 'Leo, Justin wants an opinion on the crushed leg so a decision can be made to either evacuate or operate first.'

'Tell him I'm five minutes away.'

When Abbie finished the call he continued. 'Whether I should operate or not might be semantics. Evacuation might be the only option due to staffing issues.'

Her shoulders squared, pulling her baggy scrubs across her chest and she rose on her toes. 'If the patient requires surgery before evacuation then Bandarra Base will make it possible. You worry about the surgery and let me worry about the staffing issue; that's my job.'

Her professionalism eddied around him—her sound medical judgement, the composed and or-dered way she'd run the entire emergency and the undeniable fact she'd stayed calm and focused even when she'd been pushed way out of her com-fort zone by the emergency anaesthetic.

The fact she put her patient's needs first and asked you for help, despite how you treated her.

A streak of shame assailed him. Abbie McFarlane was a damn good doctor. How the hell had he missed that last night?

Abbie's legs ached with heaviness as she sank onto the saggy couch in the staff lounge. She slipped off her shoes and swung her legs upwards, breaking the rule of no feet on the coffee table. Today had been one hell of a day but, despite her fatigue, a glow of pride warmed her. Bandarra Base had coped with a full-on emergency and, although two of their patients were in a critical

and serious condition, the fact they were still alive
lay at the feet of her team.

And Leo Costa. The opinionated, charismatic
and brilliant surgeon.

Last night she'd wanted to hate him, this morning she'd just wanted him to go as far away from
her as possible but obviously that was far too
simple a request. If the fates knew in advance
she would need a surgeon today, why couldn't
they have sent along a 'nice guy', a competent
surgeon or, better yet, a female surgeon?

But no, they were enjoying a joke at her ex-
pense and had dispatched her worst nightmare.
A man with magnetic allure, the kind of man
she'd learned was toxic to her. A couple of short
relationships at uni had made her consider perhaps she lacked judgement in her choice of men
but it had been Greg who'd really rammed home
the message. With charm and good looks, he'd
drawn her into his enticing web and then trapped
her. Now she knew to her very core that letting
a man in her life was like taking a razor blade to
her wrist—an act of self-harm.

So why, knowing all of that, did it only take
one look from those dark, dark eyes to set off
a rampaging trail of undeniable lust inside her,

sending her pulse racing and battering every single one of Greg's painful lessons about charismatic men? Battering her belief that the only way to be safe was to live a single life. A belief she hadn't questioned once in three years.

She bit her lip hard against the delicious sensations and loathed her own weakness. But, despite how she felt about her reaction to him, she couldn't deny Leo was the prize piece in today's emergency. Without him, Jenny and the elderly woman would have been immediately airlifted to Melbourne and there would have been a strong chance both of them could have died in transit. Leo had saved Jenny and given Mavis a fighting chance.

Fatigue pummelled her sitting body and Abbie fought hard to resist closing her eyes. She'd already sent Justin home and she only had to stay awake a little bit longer, do one more round and then, fingers crossed, she could go home too. The squeak of the lounge door interrupted her thoughts and, immediately on alert that a patient had deteriorated, she glanced up, expecting to see the night-nurse.

It wasn't the night-nurse. An intoxicating shimmer raced through her from the tip of her toes to the top of her scalp, leaving her breathless. Had she been blind and not able to recognise the strong brown hand that gripped the edge of the door, she would have known instantly it was Leo from the fresh mint and citrus scent that preceded him. How could a man smell so good after such a long day? 'I thought you'd gone home?'

'I spent some time with Nonna and for the last hour I've been caught up with journalists. Today's crash made it all over the news and it seems that no one could find you.' He shot her a questioning look and then walked straight to the instant hot-water heater unit and made two mugs of tea.

She shrugged, not caring that she'd left him with the press because she was pretty certain it was far more his thing than hers. 'Your patients were evacuated to Melbourne so I figured you had the time and I was still tied up with patients.'

'Well, you owe me because I've done print, radio and television interviews and I'm "mediaed" out.'

The soothing aroma of camomile wafted towards her and, for the first time since she'd walked into work hours ago, she relaxed. 'You'll look good on TV.' The words rolled out of her mouth before her exhausted brain could censor them and she gasped, wanting to grab them back.

Have you lost your mind? Warrior Abbie held her shield high over her heart, her expression incredulous.

Leo grinned—a smile full of the knowledge that not only did he know he'd look bloody fantastic on TV, he'd also heard her gaffe. A gaffe a man like Leo Costa would read as an open invitation. He stared her down. 'I didn't think you'd noticed.'

Establish distance. From the moment she'd met him she'd been cool and it was time to dig deep and find her Zen so she could cope with him and keep herself safe. She tossed her head, hating the way her curls tangled into her eyes, ruining the attempted nonchalant look. 'Let me put it this way. I noticed, and perhaps even enjoyed noticing, but not even your glossy magazine good-looks quite make up for the disrespect you showed me last night.'

She expected a tremor of anger or at the very least repressed indignation but instead he walked over to her and extended his hand.

'Hello, I'm Leo Costa, general surgeon and grandson of Maria Rossi. Pleased to meet you.'

She frowned as she swung her legs off the table and slowly raised her hand to his, all the time wondering what was actually going on. 'Abbie McFarlane.'

His firm grip wrapped around hers, under-pinned with a gentle softness that had peril writ-ten all over it. 'I hear you're the doctor who's been looking after my grandmother and you've had a few problems with one of the relatives?'

She studied his face, trying to read beyond the charm and the pretend first greeting. 'He hit ten on the difficult scale.'

His eyes widened fractionally but he didn't dis-agree as he sat down on the coffee table, directly opposite her. 'Looking back, I think he let fear for his grandmother interfere with his medical judgement.'

She hadn't expected that answer—the man had just verbalised his dread and that wasn't some-thing charismatic men usually did. 'I can under-stand the fright.'

'Well, it caught me by complete surprise. Nonna's always been so fit and well and...' He puffed out a short breath before giving a wry and apologetic smile. 'I'm sorry for what I said; I was out of line. If it makes you feel any better, my family berated me at breakfast.'

Breakfast? The word clanged in her head like a fire bell. 'Hang on; you were still insisting at nine a.m. that Maria be cared for by someone else.'

His shoulders rose as his head tilted slightly like a kid who'd been presented with the prosecuting evidence of an empty biscuit barrel. 'Stubbornness is one of my less fortunate attributes.'

Her lips twitched. 'One? So there are more?'

He captured her gaze, his eyes twinkling. 'All I will confess to is that I'm not planning on being difficult about this again. Nonna's lucky to have you; indeed Bandarra's fortunate to have a GP of your calibre, Abbie.'

She saw the captivating smile, heard the warm praise, but the bells still pealed loud in her head. 'So what you're really saying is I'm still Maria's doctor because you've realised there's no one else.'

'No. That's not what I'm saying at all.' Dismay extinguished the twinkle in his eyes and for the second time today she glimpsed a hint of the real man behind the smooth façade. 'I admit to making a snap judgement last night and I've apologised for that.'

The tic in his jaw said apologies were not something he did very often. 'But I worked alongside you today and there's no doubt you know your medicine.'

The sincerity in his voice finally satisfied her. 'Thank you.'

'You're welcome.' He moved back to the bench and carried over the tea before sitting down next to her. His firm lips curved upwards into a conspiratorial smile full of shared experiences. 'It was one hell of a day, wasn't it?'

His words matched her thoughts, which totally unnerved her. First there'd been the unexpected apology and now he appeared to want to sit and chat. That alone was enough to cope with, but added on top was his scent and aura swirling around her like an incoming tide, creating rafts of delicious sensation tickling along her veins.

He shifted his weight and the couch moved, tilting her closer to him. Silver spots danced in her head. *No, no, no.* It took every exhausted molecule to force herself to stay upright and not give in to his magnetic pull—the one that called for her to lean against his arm and lay her head on his broad shoulder. But she knew only too well that men like Leo Costa were like the foxglove plant. Pretty to look at but potentially life-threatening, and the last thing her heart needed again was life-support.

She sipped her tea, trying hard to ignore the delicious tingling on her skin and the fluttering in her stomach that sitting so close to him had activated. Warrior Abbie raised her sword across the shield. She could do this. She could sit here for a few minutes and make polite conversation because, come midnight, Leo Costa would leave her hospital. The emergency was over and they'd resolved the issue of Maria's care. She couldn't imagine him staying in Bandarra very long before Melbourne called him home, and with his departure the status quo of Bandarra Base and her much-coveted quiet life would be restored. Yes, everything would return to normal. She smiled and breathed out a long, slow, satisfying breath.

Leo sipped his tea, watching Abbie holding her cup close to her chest as if it were some sort of protective guard. An unusual cosy feeling of well-being floated through him—something he never experienced when he was in Bandarra. Could an apology really have that effect? Apparently so.

He'd always prided himself on being fair and he hadn't given Abbie the same consideration. He let the odd feeling settle over him. Today had been incredible. Not just the excitement of the 'seat-of-your-pants' surgery but working alongside Abbie. She had an air of self-containment that intrigued him. *Those eyes intrigued him.*

She stared at her shapely ankles, which rested again on the coffee table, and sighed. 'I could live without the todays of this world. We were lucky to have your expertise. Thanks.'

He was used to gushing praise but the plain appreciation had an unambiguous authenticity which he appreciated. 'I'm just glad I was here. These days I mostly do elective surgery, although I'm on the trauma roster at Melbourne City. Thankfully, I'm not always needed.'

She turned her head to look at him and understanding wove across her face, joining her cute sun-kissed freckles. 'But there's nothing quite like the buzz of a good save.'

He grinned. 'Yeah, but you can't actually go around wishing accidents on people or saying stuff like that or you sound macabre.'

She chuckled. 'You're a surgeon; it's a given.'

He tried to look affronted but instead he joined

in with her tinkling laughter. Abbie McFarlane had a straight-shooting delivery style that was as refreshing as it was unusual. He realised with a thud that apart from his immediate family, not many people spoke their mind to him any more.

She returned her gaze to her feet and he fought the urge to caress her jaw with his fingers and tilt her head back towards him so he could look into her eyes. He wanted to dive into those eyes which had stared back at him so many times today from over the top of a surgical mask, expressing everything from fear to joy.

Instead, he breathed in deeply, letting her intoxicating scent of fresh berries roll through him.

'So is this a flying visit to Bandarra?'

His libido crashed and burned as the familiar Bandarra-induced agitation spiralled through him. 'Yesterday I would have said yes. I usually fly in and fly out because I'm frantic in Melbourne.'

You keep telling yourself that's the reason. It's served you well for years. He shut his mind against the eminently reasonable voice he'd been silencing for almost as long. 'Nonna's CVA gave me a wake-up call and I want to spend a bit of time with her.'

As if in slow motion, she moved her gaze from her feet to his face, her irises widening into a reflective pool. 'Meaning?'

'I've asked my secretary to set back my patient list for the month.'

A shadow passed through her amazing eyes and her usually well-modulated voice rose slightly. 'So you're here for a few weeks?'

'Yep. Family time.' A jet of edgy unease tangoed with the flow of imposed duty. Spending time with Nonna was the right thing to do but the fact it meant spending a few weeks in Bandarra sent a shot of acid into his gut, eating at the lining. How the hell was he going to fill his days and stay sane?

He leaned back and breathed in deeply, trying to relax his chest as he stretched his arms across the back of the couch. Immediately, his fingers itched to curl around Abbie's alabaster neck and feel her softness against his skin.

Getting to know Abbie would keep the Bandarra demons at bay.

There was nothing quite like the thrill of the chase and the idea offered him the first ray of hope he'd felt since his father had demanded he stay. It would be the perfect distraction. 'I'm looking forward to spending some time with you too, now we're friends.'

Her torso shot abruptly away from the back of the couch as if she'd been electrocuted and her eyebrows shot skyward. 'Friends?' The word sounded strangled. 'That's probably going a bit far.'

Stunned surprise dumped on him like the cold and clammy touch of slime. He couldn't even think of a time when someone had rejected his overtures and the feeling stung like a wasp— sharp and painful. His jaw tensed as he tried to hold on to his good humour. 'Colleagues, then.'

She gave a tight laugh. 'We're hardly col- leagues.'

Her words bit, devaluing his interpretation of the last fourteen hours and stripping bare the memory of the camaraderie and professionalism they'd shared. 'What the hell do you call today, then?'

'Long.' She lurched to her feet, her gaze waver- ing until it finally rested on his left shoulder. 'I have to do a final round, Leo, so I'll say good- night. Thanks for your help today and enjoy your holiday in Bandarra.' She turned her back and walked away from him and towards the door.

His jaw fell open at her abrupt dismissal of
him and a curse rose to his lips, but it stalled at
the sight of her baggy scrubs moving against a
curvaceous butt. Lust collided with aggravation
and shuddered through him. His palm tingled, his
blood roared hot and he wanted to haul her back
by those caramel curls, wrap her in his arms and
demolish her prickly reserve with a kiss.

For the first time in months his body came
alive—every colour seemed brighter, every feeling more intense and he buzzed with the wonder
of it. He didn't know if it was the aftermath of
the sheer rush of the emergency or the challenge
of the very brisk Abbie McFarlane but, either
way, if he had to stay in Bandarra he had to keep
busy. Seducing Abbie McFarlane would be the
perfect distraction. He clapped his hands as the
seeds of a plan started to shoot. This was going
to be too much fun and Abbie McFarlane didn't
stand a chance.

CHAPTER FOUR

ABBIE let Murphy, her Border collie, pull her along the path, totally oblivious to the usually soothing gnarled river red-gums with their silver and grey bark. Not even the majestic sight of fifteen pelicans coming in to land on the blue-brown river water could haul her mind away from the fact that Leo Costa was staying in Bandarra.

She gave a half-laugh tinged with madness that had Murphy looking up at her, his tawny-gold eyes quizzical. She'd been dreading Justin leaving, knowing that her workload would double. Now that seemed like a saving grace because she'd be so flat out virtually living at the clinic and the hospital that she'd never have any time in town to run into Leo. Who knew work would save her?

The magpies' early morning call drifted towards her and she heard a message in the flute-like song. Work had saved her before. Greg might have stripped her of everything else, but he hadn't been able to take away her job. She'd survived and rebuilt her independence. Never again would she confuse lust with love, charm for affection, or control for care. Now she had the unconditional love of a dog, which she'd choose every single time over the pile of broken promises men left in their wake.

'Come on, Murph, time for breakfast at the clinic.' She broke into a jog, channelling all her energies into the run, driving away every unsettling thought of an onyx-eyed man with broad shoulders that hinted at being able to shelter those he loved from the world.

The clinic was in the hospital grounds and housed in the original Bandarra hospital which had been lovingly restored in its centennial year. With its high gabled roof, tall chimneys and cream-painted decorative timber, it welcomed patients with its sweeping veranda and kangaroo motifs worked lovingly into the mosaic floor. Abbie had seen an old photo from 1908 where a hammock hung on the veranda so she'd bought a brightly coloured hammock and had slung it between the last two posts on the front veranda. One day she planned to have time to lie in it for more than the brief 'test' she'd taken when she'd installed it. Meanwhile Murphy enjoyed lying underneath it, using it as shade.

The thick brick walls always offered a respite from the heat. 'Morning, Debbie,' Abbie called to her practice nurse as she made her way into the cool kitchen, her stomach rumbling at the thought of fresh grapes just off the vine combined with locally made yoghurt drizzled with honey. 'Where's Jessica?'

Debbie followed her into the kitchen. 'She's come down with a filthy cold so I'm afraid we're juggling reception and patients today.'

Abbie groaned. 'That's a great start to being one doctor down. Has anything come from the board about a new appointee?' She dropped thick slices of crusty bakery bread into the toaster.

'Robert Gleeson said he's had applications from Egypt, India and Kenya and he'd be catching up with you soon for interview times.'

Abbie sighed. Rural medicine seemed to only attract doctors with the 'short-term' in mind and then they left just as she'd trained them up. The thought reminded her that yesterday's emergency had got in the way of a farewell. 'Is Justin able to have his party tonight?'

Debbie shook her head sadly. 'He's set to leave

this morning but I'm sure he'll call by first. Meanwhile, I got in early and pulled the histories for the first patients and my diabetic clinic doesn't start until ten so I can woman the phones.'

She smiled. 'Thanks, Debbie, and thanks for keeping things ticking over here yesterday while I was tied up at the hospital all day. You have no idea what a load you take off me with your clinics, which reminds me, the funding came through for your "travelling pap test" clinic, so well done on that too.'

Debbie beamed with the praise before dashing out to answer the phone, leaving Abbie alone to eat her breakfast. The next time she was alone was four hours later when the morning session finally wrapped up. 'Debbie, I'm grabbing lunch from Tony's; do you want me to get you anything?'

The practice nurse stuck her head out of the treatment room. 'I'm set, thanks, and Eli Jenkins is here for his ulcer treatment. Can you check the fax? I just heard it beep at reception.'

Abbie's head was already spinning from hunger. She had a huge afternoon ahead of her and all she could think of right now was one of Tony's focaccias and a mug of his creamy latte—he refused to serve it in a glass, saying it was a travesty to good coffee. 'It won't be anything urgent. I'll read it when I get back.'

The heat hit her the moment she opened the heavy red-gum door and she automatically reached for her sunhat, which she always hung on the coat-stand. She loved making sure the clinic had an 'at home' welcoming feel to it and the hat-stand was part of that, as was the umbrella stand with its stash of umbrellas. Not that they got used very often as it had been ages since Bandarra had seen rain. Moths would probably fly out if a patient opened one.

Usually Murphy raced to the door to meet her, ever hopeful of a walk, no matter how short, but his smiling face wasn't waiting for her. She glanced down the long veranda, ready to call her dog, but Murphy's name died on her lips as her mouth dried to a crisp.

Lying in her hammock, and looking for all the world as if he belonged there, was Leo. His long and tanned shorts-clad legs stretched out in front of him, and one arm was crooked behind the back of his head, the angle moulding his soft cotton designer T-shirt tight to the well defined muscles of his chest and shoulders. Aviator sun-glasses covered his onyx eyes while his other long-fingered surgeon's hand dangled lazily over the hammock's side, stroking Murphy's head.

The Border collie looked up adoringly while his tail thumped out an enthusiastic tattoo.

Turncoat!

Hot and cold streaked through Abbie, making her tremble and sending her already spinning head into a vortex spiral where hunger, lust and fast-fading common sense got sucked in together. *Danger—stay strong.* She dragged in a deep and steadying breath. If she ignored him, she could pretend he wasn't here. She slapped her thigh and called her dog. 'Murphy, here, boy.'

The dog turned his black and white head and smiled at her as if to say, *Look who I found; come meet him too.*

Leo rose elegantly from the hammock, in total contrast to the inelegant way Abbie had fallen out of it the day she'd tried, and he walked up the veranda towards her with her dog trotting besottedly by his side. She wanted to hate him but really she only hated her reaction to him. A reaction she must master.

His smile lit up the air around him, although the slight aura of tension she'd occasionally glimpsed hovered. 'Hello, Abbie. Great dog; is he yours?'

She nodded and, knowing she couldn't ignore him, she chose the direct approach—the one that usually made her sound brisk and officious and had very occasionally sent interns scurrying. 'What are you doing here, Leo?'

He didn't even blink at the bald words. Instead, he tilted his head and met her gaze with a friendly and open expression. 'I thought we could have lunch together.'

No way. 'I don't think so. I'm just grabbing a quick focaccia before afternoon clinic.' She turned away from him and staring straight ahead, determined not to look at him, she started walking towards town.

'Me too.' Leo fell easily into step beside her.

The scent of laundry powder mixed in with healthy masculine sweat encircled her, fuzzing her brain. 'Why do you need a quick lunch when surely the point of being on holiday is being able to have a long lunch?'

'Afternoon clinic starts at two, right?'

Her head snapped sideways so fast she felt something rip. 'It does, but why does that concern you?'

His friendly smile suddenly became wide and knowing. 'I hate being late.'

She felt her brows draw down towards the bridge of her nose and heard her mother's warning voice shriek, *wrinkles*. She batted the voice away, needing all her concentration to stay on top of what was going on. He surely didn't look sick; in fact he looked decadently healthy, and yesterday's fatigue which had played around his eyes had completely vanished. Today he looked relaxed and gorgeous. Dangerously gorgeous. 'Do you have an appointment?'

A ripple of unexpected confusion skated across his usually confident face. 'Robert Gleeson should have told you this morning.'

Her throat tightened at the hospital CEO's name and every nerve-ending fired off a mass alert. 'Told me what?'

'That I'm doing half days to help out until the new doctor is appointed.'

Silver spots danced in front of her eyes. *Leo working in the clinic.* Oh, God, that was probably what the fax she'd so cheerfully ignored had been about. Jumbled thoughts tumbled off her lips. 'But you're on holiday to spend time with your family.' She heard her rising voice, the words tinged with slight hysteria. 'Surely you don't want a busman's holiday?'

He shrugged, but it seemed overly casual, as if he'd had to try hard to achieve the effect. 'I can do both. Robert contacted me this morning after getting yesterday's report and seeing all the media attention. He thought it would help you out and it suits me. I like to keep busy.'

She grasped at straws but they seemed lined with slippery mud. 'But you're a surgeon.'

Intelligent eyes fixed her with a piercing look. 'So what are you saying? That I can't cut it as a GP?'

The mud threatened to dump right on top of her and she opted for the easy jibe. 'There's a lot of listening and not much cutting. You'll be bored rigid after one session.'

Two jet-black brows rose, disappearing under a thatch of thick hair. 'That's a big statement based on nothing much at all. Are you always this quick to judge?'

His words hit with painful accuracy and sliced open guilt. Yesterday he'd been great with his patients and she couldn't fault that but she didn't trust herself working with him. 'I just meant that the work won't be the high-powered stuff you're used to.'

He crossed his arms across a powerful chest.

'Maybe I can make a dent in the waiting list Robert was talking about, seeing as you only get a visiting surgeon once a month. Like I said, I like to keep busy.'

The reality of the waiting list duelled with the sheer panic that bubbled furiously inside her at the thought of working with Leo. Of staying safe and not being tempted to go down a self-destructive path. *Remember Greg.* But the waiting list issue was bigger than her and the hardworking people of Bandarra had enough to contend with from the tough climatic and economic conditions of the area. They deserved the unexpected advantage of a surgeon in their midst for a few weeks, even if Leo Costa's charisma scared her witless.

She swallowed hard and forced up the words that needed to be said. 'I'll take you up on that.'

He clapped his hands. 'On lunch? Excellent.'

Charm played on his high cheekbones, both enticing and inviting, and deep inside Abbie a tiny crack widened. How much danger could there possibly be in sitting down for a quick focaccia?

Plenty. Warrior Abbie raised her shield. *This is work.*

She cleared her throat and shored up her determination to keep Leo Costa a solid distance away from her, both physically and emotionally. She pasted on her professional smile. 'I'll take you up on the offer of reducing the waiting list. In fact I'll pull out the files and we can prioritise a list. How does that sound?'

He nodded agreeably. 'It sounds fine.'

But there was something about the timbre of his voice and the easy smile that played on his lips that had Abbie regretting the whole idea. Leo Costa working in Bandarra might be good medicine for the town but it was a health hazard for her.

Leo strode from the clinic towards the hospital on his way to visit Nonna before his planning meeting with Abbie. With Debbie's able assistance, Leo's first session had been remarkably smooth and, although he'd seen a lot of patients, he hadn't seen anything of Abbie. It had been on the tip of his tongue to suggest they take their meeting over dinner but that would only give her another excuse to say no and she was extremely good at that. He couldn't remember the last time he'd had to work so hard at getting a date but her 'no's' just made him more determined and inventive. He'd rung Anna's restaurant and ordered an antipasti platter and a bottle of wine so they could meet and eat at the clinic, and he might just be able to break down that intriguing wall of aloofness she was so good at building.

'*Ciao*, Nonna, *com stai?*'

Nonna raised her hand and smiled. 'Leopoldo. When am I going home?'

'You have to ask Abbie that, Nonna. I promised her I wouldn't interfere.'

Nonna's perceptive gaze instantly turned curious but that didn't hide the lining of reproach. 'You've broken promises to women before.'

He sighed and rubbed his chin, realising he'd just unwittingly stepped into a topic he usually did his best to avoid. Nonna had taken his divorce from Christina personally and it was the only thing about him and his life where she actively voiced disappointment. It amazed him that she should be so angry with him over a failed marriage and yet never blame him for Dom's death when the cause lay so squarely at his feet. But perhaps she did blame him because Dom and Christina were inextricably linked and always would be.

'So, Maria, I've got good new—' Abbie

breezed into the ward, a white coat covering a crumpled pair of knee-length khaki shorts and a white blouse that begged for the touch of a hot iron. Her green eyes widened as if she'd taken a jolt of electricity.

'Leo.' A ripple of tension wove through her from the top of her sun-kissed caramel curls, down and around pert breasts, across a nipped-in waist, before spinning around curvaceous legs and disappearing into the floor. 'I thought you were still at the clinic.'

Leo deciphered the code as, *If I'd known you were here I wouldn't have come,* and annoyance fizzed in his veins. He'd apologised for his behaviour and she'd accepted so surely their rugged start was now water under the bridge. So why did she want to avoid him so much? It fuelled his determination to cut a swathe through her reserve. He gave her a slow smile. 'I finished the list and cut out early to visit Nonna so I wouldn't be late for our meeting.'

'Oh, right, of course.' Her hands seemed to flutter as she reached for the chart, the action unusually flustered.

Then he caught a flash of something flare in her eyes before being quickly replaced by her professional doctor look—the one she always gave to him. He stifled his grin and mentally high-fived. Abbie McFarlane was working seriously hard to stay aloof. Wine and antipasti might just do the trick.

'Actually, Leo, it's good you're here.' With studied casualness she turned back to Maria. 'I know you want to go home and you've been recovering well but I want you to have some time in rehab, and a bed's just come up. Leo can transfer you now and that way you're ready for physio and OT first thing tomorrow.'

Maria beamed and patted Abbie's hand. 'I will walk there.'

Abbie shook her head. 'Sorry, Maria, but you have to go in a wheelchair; it's hospital policy. But once you're in the rehab ward you'll be able to use your frame.'

The old woman gave a snort of derision and Leo expected a tirade of rapid-fire Italian to follow but his grandmother surprised him. 'Leopoldo, pack my things. *Dottore*, get my dress.'

Abbie looked startled for a moment and Leo wondered if she'd refuse the request or call a nurse but, as his hand opened a drawer, she walked to the wardrobe. Three dresses hung neatly and, without giving Maria a choice, she plucked one off the rack. 'This will do nicely.'

Leo hid his smile. He'd learned early that he did things Nonna wanted but in his own way. Abbie had worked that out fast.

Ten minutes later, with Maria seated in the wheelchair, Leo pushing and Abbie carrying the small suitcase, they crossed the courtyard to the rehab wing.

'When I am home, *dottore*, you need to come again and make bread.'

'Maria, my last attempt was a disaster. It was so rock-hard that if it was thrown it could knock a man unconscious.'

Leo laughed. 'Remind me never to upset you in a kitchen.'

Abbie crooked a challenging eyebrow and lights sparked in her eyes. 'No chance of that ever happening.' She bent her head towards Maria. 'Kitchens and I have never been a match and never will be. I know enough to feed myself and that's all I need to know.'

'Pfft.' Maria threw her hands out in front of her as if Abbie had just uttered a cardinal sin. 'Food is not just for a hungry belly. It feeds the soul.'

Abbie's expression clouded for a moment before

her shoulders rolled back and she picked up her pace.

Leo's gaze swept over Abbie's slight but shapely body that had curves in all the right places. Abbie wasn't underfed but he'd noticed occasional shadows peeking from those amazing eyes, and his observant *nonna* had noticed too. Abbie hadn't realised that Nonna wasn't trying to teach her to cook but was trying to teach her the joy of food.

Abbie opened the rehab ward door. 'Here we are.'

Maria's orders started flowing again in a combination of English and Italian and she didn't pause until they'd settled her into the dining room. They left her happily chatting with the other residents and her final words to their retreating backs were, 'Hang my clothes.'

Leo strode into Nonna's new room. Shaking his head in a combination of half laughter and half apology, he opened the wardrobe door. 'And that was Nonna in full flight.'

'True, she organises us mere mortals.' Abbie passed him clothes from the suitcase, a wicked laugh twitching her plump lips. 'But who knew that the hotshot city surgeon is a complete pushover when it comes to his grandmother?'

He slid the coat hanger over the metal rail and grinned. 'Not many people know that. It's classified information.'

Sea-green eyes, devoid of any shadows or clouds, twinkled brightly with teasing in their depths. 'Classified information? How so?'

He winked at her. 'I've got a reputation to protect.'

Her belly laugh brought a delicious pink to her cheeks. 'Are you worried that if the information got out it might put a dent in your macho surgeon image?'

He hung up the last dress and turned to face her, a streak of fun pouring through him unlike anything he'd felt in months. 'Let me put it this way—if word got out I might not be responsible for my actions.'

She chuckled as she leaned against the wardrobe door, her arms crossed firmly against her chest. 'Oh, right, and if I talk, what are you going to do to me? Hit me with that high wattage charm that works for you so well? I hate to tell you, Romeo, but it won't ever work on me.'

Her words laid down a challenge he couldn't refuse. Raising his left arm, he pressed it against the door, leaving plenty of space for her to duck out underneath, should she choose that option. Leaning in closer, he kept his gaze fixed firmly on her face as her strawberry and liquorice scent swirled around him, filling his lungs before pouring through him and leaving a trail of banked heat.

He caught a flicker of movement—the twitch of a muscle in her cheek. A chink in her professed armour? Perhaps she wasn't as impervious to him as she made out. Slowly he brought his right hand up to her face, twirling a tight curl around his finger as he spoke softly. 'And what makes you so sure?'

She tilted her chin, the action all defiance. 'I've been charmed by experts and I know every trick in the book.'

He'd expected her to spin out under his arm and stalk away but instead she stood her ground, so he edged in closer until he could feel the heat of her body radiating out to meet him and the tickle of her sweet breath on his face. 'But you don't know all my tricks.'

She swallowed hard and heat unfurled inside him so fast he thought he'd ignite. A pulse quivered against the pale skin of her throat, completely undoing him, and with a groan he gave in and lowered his mouth to hers.

Plump lips of pillow-softness met his with complete stillness, but the hint of sweet sultana grapes and summer sunshine hovered, pleading to be tasted. He flicked his tongue, stealing the tang, wanting the full taste.

Her arms stayed crossed against her chest like an unyielding barrier and her eyes were squeezed shut as if she was battling herself. He almost pulled back but then she gave a moan-like sigh and opened her lips to him.

His tongue tumbled over the precipice and the taste of summer fruits flooded his mouth. Their sweetness bubbled through his veins like champagne—intoxicating and demanding—and he angled his mouth, seeking more.

Her tongue met his with a jolt and immediately darted away, only to return a moment later, all hesitancy gone. With the experienced mouth of a temptress, she took her full taste of him and at the same time branded him with her own unique essence.

White lights exploded in his head and his blood pounded to his groin with an urgency he hadn't known in months. Pure lust poured through him, driving all of his actions as every cell in his body screamed to touch her, feel her, taste her and fill her with himself. Frustratingly, her arms still stayed rigidly between them, acting like a blockade and preventing him from lining his body against hers. Instead, he slid his free hand up into her hair, the silky strands caressing his palms and releasing their heady scent of floral fragrance.

She tilted her head back and her throaty groan rocked through him. The realisation that buried under those chain-store clothes lay the body and soul of an incredibly sexual woman socked him so hard it threatened to undo him on the spot in a way that hadn't happened since he was fifteen. He gently nipped her lip and she replied in kind and the last vestiges of reason floated away. Sound vanished, light wavered and he lost himself to everything except the overwhelming need to have that amazing mouth on and in his.

Abbie floated on layers of glorious sensation, totally disconnected to her real world and lost in the wondrous touch of Leo's mouth on hers, trailing along her jaw and down into the sweet hollow of her throat. His mouth suckled, nipped, tasted and branded her, filling her with swirling light and colour. Colour that built upon itself until it detonated inside her, sending a surging torrent of unmitigated lust rolling through her, leaving no part of her untouched.

Her body took over—seeking pleasure, needing it like it needed oxygen. Her breasts strained at the lace of her bra, her hips tilted forward and her protective arms fell to her sides, their barrier utterly vanquished.

The gap between them vanished. His legs pressed against the length of hers, her hips melded with his, her breasts flattened against his solid chest and their combined heat roared into a fire ball of heat-seeking bliss. He absorbed her moan of spiralling need with his mouth, as her hand tugged its way under his shirt, desperate to touch him. Her palm hit the corded musculature of his back, his skin burning hers, and her fingers went exploring, trailing the length of his spine before burying themselves in his thick hair.

The scent of desire cloaked them, tongues duelled, neither able to get enough of the other and then his hand cupped her breast, his thumb skimming across the utilitarian cotton of her blouse, caressing the erect nub so desperate for his touch.

'*Sei magnifica.*'

Leo's usually velvet voice rasped out the words with the grazing sound of gravel, instantly slicing through Abbie's lust-fuelled haze. The hard corner of the wardrobe door bit sharply into her back, Leo's weight pressed heavily against her, as did his arousal, and the shock snapped her eyes wide open.

Everything came into sharp focus. The windows of the rehab ward, the two neatly made patients' beds with their smart green covers and the white porcelain of the hand basin. Deep inside her, a wobbly Warrior Abbie stumbled to her feet, picked up her sword and shield and screamed in horror. *What the hell are you doing? Remember your pact. Staying single is the only safe way.*

Reality dumped so hard on Abbie she could hardly move her ribcage to breathe and her legs struggled to hold her up. She was wrapped around Leo like a sex-starved teenager, a hair's breadth away from locking her legs up high around his waist and impaling herself against him, letting him have sex with her against a wardrobe door in his grandmother's room at the rehab ward.

Oh, God, how had she let this happen? Since

Greg she'd decided to take a totally different path in her life and she wasn't going backwards, yet look what she'd just done. Horrified, she pulled her hands out from under his shirt and dragged her mouth away from his. Somehow, despite her panting chest, she managed to force out, 'That kiss is never happening again.'

Dark eyes filled with the fog of lust stared back at her. 'No, you're right.'

'I am?' Bewilderment lost out to relief. Thank God he knew it was a mistake as well. She tugged at her blouse, straightening it. 'I mean good. I'm glad we agree.'

His finger reached out and tucked a curl behind her ear. 'That kiss has passed and can never be repeated because no kiss is ever the same twice.' Impossibly, his eyes darkened even more. 'Still, it will be fun to test that theory in a more appropriate place.'

Panic lurched through her. 'No. What I meant was *we* are never kissing again.'

He looked at her with a gaze of incredulity. 'Abbie, given what just went down between us, not kissing again would be an absolute tragedy.'

She pushed past him, needing to put a bigger space between them, needing to do everything in her power to remove the temptation that was Leo Costa. 'Famine, disease and death are a tragedy, Leo. Lust is just a nuisance that can be controlled.'

His black brows hit his hair line. 'A nuisance?'

But she wasn't being drawn back into dangerous Leo-filled waters that involved discussing anything other than work. 'Yes, a nuisance. We're colleagues for the next few weeks, Leo. As professionals, I'm sure we can keep our hands off each other and focus on the health of Bandarra.'

Leo's palm slapped the wardrobe door closed and he turned towards her with a lazy smile but shadows lurked in his eyes. 'I have every intention of focusing on the health of Bandarra.'

His words should have reassured her but it was what he didn't say that worried her.

CHAPTER FIVE

LEO walked into the kitchen to find Anna standing at the coffee machine frothing milk for the breakfast cappuccinos. He was grumpy and out of sorts after a night spent fighting the sheets more than sleeping in them. His sleep had been a tangled mess of the usual demon dreams but added in was Abbie's mouth, so hot and delicious against his own one minute and gone the next. 'This morning I need espresso.'

His sister's dark brown eyes gazed at him with a speculative look. 'Too much Cab Sav last night, big brother?'

'I was working late, not drinking.' Leo grimaced and slid into the chair remembering how Abbie had changed the venue of their meeting from the clinic to the hospital and had deliberately sat at the furthest end of the very long hospital boardroom table. They'd discussed possible surgery cases over the travesty that was instant coffee, while the food and wine he'd ordered lay untouched at the clinic.

He'd spent the first two cases struggling to reconcile the distant cool professional opposite him with the exciting and uninhibited woman who'd kissed him so wholeheartedly and without restraint in his grandmother's ward. He hadn't been that turned on since— His mind blanked. He couldn't recall the last time he'd been so aroused. Then she'd coolly stepped back from him and hit him with her calm and uncompromising gaze. It was as if she'd flicked an internal switch and had locked down every single one of her sexual feelings. The fact she'd called the most wondrous of life's sensations 'a nuisance' had totally floored him.

Anna slid an espresso cup under the machine. 'Work? Is that what you call it now? I saw your order at the restaurant and it screamed "seduction plan". Which nurse was it this time?'

He grunted. 'I told you, I was working and it took forever. Abbie McFarlane must have pulled out the files of every possible candidate for surgery between here and Budjerree.' If he had to stay in Bandarra then at least he'd be busy.

Anna laughed. 'I told you, Abbie's a dynamo doctor.'

She's a dynamo kisser.

The wire door thwacked back on its hinges and thundering feet sounded on the floorboards, interrupting his thoughts. Leo turned to see Anna's eleven-year-old twin girls—broad brimmed hats on their heads and green school bags on their backs—charge into the room. The same age when he and Dom had been inseparable.

'Uncle Leo.' The girls threw themselves at him, their eyes wide with wonder. 'Nonna Rosa said you're staying for a long holiday.'

Leo opened his arms, hugging them harder than he should as he forced memories down. 'Well, for a little while.'

Donna, the eldest by five minutes and who'd tried to be first at everything ever since, begged, 'Can you play tennis with me after school?'

It will keep you busy.

Lauren snuggled in closer. 'I need you to pitch softballs to me so I can get really good at hitting home runs.'

'*Stelline mie*, I can do both. In fact I can even come and see you play in your competitions on Saturday.'

They squealed in delight and hugged him hard.

Anna clapped her hands. 'Girls, outside now or you'll miss the bus. Go.'

They kissed their mother on the cheek and, with calls of 'bye' and 'ciao', the door slammed shut behind them.

Anna passed Leo his coffee and sat down with hers, her face filled with surprise.

Her expression ate into him, along with his general agitation. 'What?'

'Sorry, I'm just astounded that you offered to watch the girls play.'

'Why wouldn't I?' He heard the aggravation in his voice and took in a deep breath.

She shrugged. 'Because you're always tense and distracted when you're here.'

He ran his hand across the back of his neck, wanting to deny her accusation, but he could not. 'I'm usually only here for a day or two but this trip I have the time.' *Way too much time.*

'Well, it's good you're staying longer. Mamma's beside herself. You should have seen her in town yesterday. She must have stopped every second person to tell them you were working here for a month. Do you realise you haven't spent more than two days at a time in Bandarra since you left for uni years ago?'

He knew that was exactly how it had been because it was a deliberate decision on his part. Being in Bandarra ate at him like acid, reminding him of Christina and Dom and taunting him with his success in life when Dom hadn't had a chance to excel. Reminding him that he'd stuffed up two lives. He matched her casual shrug. 'I'm a specialist surgeon and it keeps me in Melbourne.'

Anna reached out her hand and in an uncharacteristic gesture she patted his arm. 'It means a lot to Mamma and Papà. It's not often all four of their kids are under the same roof.'

Five kids. He bit off the comment he so wanted to shout but instead he forced a wry smile to his lips. 'Oh, yeah, just like growing up, except for the three sons-in-law and eight grandchildren.'

'At least your sisters have given Mamma and Nonna the family crowd they love.' Her hand touched his in sisterly concern. 'What happened with Christina was a long time ago. I heard she's remarried and teaching school now in Italy. But what about you, bro? It's time you tried again.'

You only married me to hold on to Dom. I won't put up with your resentment any more. Christina's bitter words boomed in his head as if it had only been yesterday. As his mouth opened to say, *No way am I trying again,* Abbie's caramel curls and plump red lips suddenly beamed across his brain in brilliant 3D. *What the hell?* Abbie McFarlane was one sexy woman but he didn't do 'forever' with any woman. He'd tried and let Christina down badly. Just like he'd let Dom down. He wasn't ever doing that to anyone again and that was why he excelled in short-term superficial relationships. Fun, uncomplicated good times and then he moved on, but he always made sure every woman knew the ground rules before the first date.

He drained his coffee, not wanting to have this conversation. 'I'm leaving all the family stuff to you, Chiara and Bianca because you do it so much better than me.' He pushed back his chair and grabbed a brioche off the plate. 'I better not be late for clinic. Ciao.'

He ignored the sigh of frustration that came from his sister's lips and headed out the door into a clear and hot day. A normal February day with the early morning song of the magpies floating across the warm air. The kids of the vineyard's employees shot past on bikes, a plume of red dust rising behind their wheels as they raced towards the main road, late for school. He and Dom had done the same thing every morning, racing each other to the gate.

A sudden pain burned hot under his sternum and he rubbed it with his left hand. Damn it. Day three in Bandarra and already it was too hard. Spinning on his heel, he marched towards his rental car, thankful that clinic started in ten minutes and he had a surgical list to prioritise. Not to mention his pursuit of Abbie McFarlane. A ticking sexual time bomb lay under her frumpy clothes and he intended to be the man to detonate it.

Abbie tried unsuccessfully to out-stride Leo as their paths intersected on the way to the operating theatre but he easily caught her up.

'Abbie, you can walk with me; I promise I won't bite.' He grinned. 'That is, unless you want me to.'

His deep voice streamed over her like rich, dark melted chocolate and it took every ounce of strength not to lick her lips and replay their kiss. Her body wanted him so badly it constantly hummed with need but her head and heart knew better, so she kept walking and answered briskly, 'I had no idea surgeons had such a sense of humour.'

'More than some GPs, it seems.' He shoved his hands deep into his pockets. 'Come on, Abbie, we're colleagues; let's eat lunch together.'

She shook her head emphatically. 'No.'

'Dinner at the best table in my sister's award-winning restaurant?'

The idea tempted her. She'd wanted to eat at Mia Casa for ages. 'No, thank you.'

'Coffee at Tony's under a market umbrella?'

'Uh-uh.'

Leo didn't miss a beat. 'OK, then, popcorn and chocolate at the latest chick-flick blockbuster?'

She laughed. 'Now you're getting desperate.'

His eyes had the temerity to twinkle, making her stomach lurch. He gave a fluid shrug as if all her 'no's' just slid off his broad, broad shoulders. 'I appreciate all genres of film.'

She wanted to scoff but sincerity lined the edges of his eyes and bracketed his mouth, and that dis-armed her. She wanted to put Leo Costa into a predictable box but more often than not he just didn't fit.

'If you want to be more active, then how about a bike ride and a picnic?'

'In this heat? Are you insane?'

'Not that I'm aware of, no.' The scar on his chin seemed to suddenly whiten as his jaw stiffened for a fraction of a second. 'We could do it early in the morning or at sunset.'

'I walk Murphy then.' Even to her ears that excuse sounded lame.

'I suppose I should be thankful you didn't say "washing my hair".' He crossed his arms. 'So, basically, no matter what I suggest you're going to say no?'

She nodded. 'Now you're getting the idea.'

'That's hardly in the collegiate spirit.' His voice held not unreasonable criticism.

She sighed. Her body tingled and was busy yelling 'yes' to every invitation but fear kept her saying 'no'. After yesterday's major lapse, she knew exactly what would happen if she said yes to any invitation that threw the two of them together on their own—she'd end up in his arms and probably in his bed, hating herself and hating him. Saying no was her only option.

Leo suddenly stopped in front of the OR doors,

effectively blocking them. 'Do you want me to stop asking you out?'

'Thank you.' The words shot out on a breath of relief.

'Hang on, I asked you if you wanted me to stop; I didn't actually agree to it.' His smile was all charm and appeal. 'How's this for an idea? You invite *me* to something and then I'll quit asking you out.'

She rushed to say, *But that's still you getting your own way*, when her brain actually engaged and she clamped her lips shut. This was perfect. She could invite him out to something where there'd be no chance of them being alone—in fact they'd be surrounded by ten kids from the shelter. This was the ideal solution because, not only would it stop him asking her out, she actually needed an extra adult to help run the programme.

Warrior Abbie armed her sword across her shield and Abbie stared straight into his handsome face—staring down danger because now she had the protection she needed. 'So you'll come along to whatever I ask you to?'

'Sure, why not? I'm up for anything.'

She tilted her head, her gaze sweeping his

gorgeous and toned body. 'It might involve your designer clothes getting dirty.'

'No problem. I grew up in the country, remember. I can get down and dirty with the best of them.'

He winked at her and his face creased into deep, warm laughter lines. The combination of his dark eyes and black stubble radiated a wave of pure, unadulterated sex appeal that rocked into Abbie so hard she broke out into a hot and tingling sweat. Warrior Abbie fanned herself with her shield.

Oh come on, we can withstand sex appeal and cheap innuendo.

'Tell me what it is, then.' His words sounded impatient and his urbane charm slipped slightly.

She caught a flash—a remnant—of an enthusiastic and guileless, excited little boy. No sex appeal at all. Her heart hiccoughed. *No, no, no.* She tossed her head and rearmed. 'Well, it involves a sense of adventure, a good sense of humour and working with kids. Do you think you qualify?'

'*Sì.* Absolutely. I love kids.'

Her heart lurched again. She loved kids too and had wanted a child of her own but that dream had been discarded, along with her tattered dreams of happy families. Now she worked with kids from the shelter, completely understanding their bewilderment at how their family life had suddenly been turned upside down.

'Great. Then meet me tomorrow night at the old jetty for canoeing on the river.'

Like water connecting with flames, the twinkling light in his eyes doused. The hovering tension that often surrounded him zoomed back in, firmly front and centre, and all traces of the charismatic man vanished. 'I can't do that.'

Abbie blinked in surprise at his steely tone as an irrational and unwanted streak of disappointment shot through her. 'But you just said you're up for anything.'

His tanned skin tightened across his high cheekbones as his left hand brushed the scar on his chin. 'I have to scrub.' Without another word, he disappeared through the door.

Abbie's feet stayed still as if glued to the floor while her head spun, dizzy with unanswered questions. What had just happened? She couldn't match up the flirting charm with the man who'd just walked away from her. She'd seen Leo in action wearing many guises—the determined grandson, the calm professional and talented surgeon, the super-smooth playboy—but she'd never imagined he'd be a man who'd just walk away from something.

It's no big deal, it's just canoeing. Perhaps he had a prior engagement and the timing clashed? What did it matter that he'd said no? She should be relieved and happy. She'd kept her side of the bargain and issued the invitation, which meant he had to honour his promise of not asking her out. This was a totally win-win situation for her.

But the relief she knew she should feel didn't come. If his 'no' was to do with not being available then surely he would have said so instead of walking away. And he had walked away.

He'd said he loved kids so it wasn't that. A gazillion questions zoomed around in her head as she tried to work out his uncharacteristic behaviour but she couldn't fathom any reason for it. It made no sense and yet something about canoeing had made him turn pale and turn on his heel.

Her beeper sounded and she snapped her attention back to work. A patient was waiting for her to administer a general anaesthetic and that came ahead of an enigmatic surgeon. At least it did for now.

* * *

Leo stripped off his gloves and dropped them into the bin. The cholecystectomy he'd just performed had been straightforward and uneventful and now the patient was in recovery. As the surgeon, he should be filled with a sense of satisfaction at a job well done. Instead, he kept thinking about how he'd almost lost the plot when Abbie had invited him canoeing.

Several times during the course of the operation he'd caught her staring at him over the top of her mask. Usually he welcomed the gaze of a beautiful woman, loving how much flirting could take place with eyes alone when the rest of the face was hidden. But today there'd been no flirting and he'd found himself ducking her penetrating and insightful stare, hating the fact that his guard had not merely slipped but had plummeted and smashed to pieces at the mention of the river.

Being in Bandarra was bad enough but using the river—that was something he'd never do.

He'd been thankful that as the surgeon he could leave the theatre earlier than the anaesthetist, which meant Abbie was still tied up in Recovery and not able to verbalise all the questions he'd seen flashing in her eyes. But, no matter how many questions she had, he didn't talk about

Dom to anyone—not even Nonna—and he had no plans to start talking now.

Damn it, why had he even suggested she ask him out on a promise he'd stop asking her out? He'd thought it such a clever idea, a way to spend time with Abbie on her own turf, gambling on a bigger chance that she'd relax some of those barriers she held up so hard and high. Relax them and lower them so they could resume that kiss. That mind-blowing, blood-pounding kiss that had planted a craving deep inside him which burned like an eternal flame seeking more fuel. But the idea had bitten him hard, leaving his game plan frayed and exposing a part of his life he kept very deeply buried.

He pushed his way out through the double doors, needing to concentrate on doing his final job as the surgeon and keep all thoughts of the past at bay.

'*Buon giorno,* Sofia. The operation went very well and Lorenzo will be back eating your wonderful *zuppa* in no time.'

'*Grazie*, Leo.' Sofia, a younger friend of his Nonna's, pinched his cheek. 'You are a good boy and a talented man. You must come soon and eat with us in the Cantina while you are home.'

Home. He knew there was no advantage in pointing out he'd lived in Melbourne for a year longer than he'd ever lived in Bandarra. Country towns never completely let their favourite sons go, no matter how much they wanted to be gone. He also knew there was no point in refusing the invitation because a 'no' would not be accepted.

'That would be lovely, Sofia.'

'Good. My granddaughter, she is a good cook; I think you should meet her.'

Good cook or not, Leo didn't want to be matched up. 'I'll bring a friend who can enjoy her cooking as well.' He spoke the protective words with no friend in mind but he immediately heard Abbie's voice in his head. *I know enough to feed myself and that's all I need to know.*

The thought of watching Abbie's lush lips close around a slice of the delectable wood-fire pizza that Sofia was famous for, and being next to her the moment she made the connection that food wasn't just for sating hunger, jolted him with heat.

'*Bene.*' Sofia tried not to look too disappointed as she walked towards the ward to wait for Lorenzo.

Leo puffed out a breath, his duty done. Unless

the nursing staff paged him, he wasn't required at the hospital or the clinic until tomorrow. The afternoon stretched before him—him and Bandarra—the thought sent a restlessness to him. He could go home but his parents' house would be empty and he wanted to avoid a quiet and censorious house.

La Bella winery thrived because of hard work. His father would be in the vineyard but, ever since Stefano's decree that Leo stay for the vintage, Leo had made sure he was never alone with his father because he anticipated a conversation he didn't want to have. A tour bus was booked in and his mother and younger sisters would be busy at the cellar door and Anna would be directing lunch at the restaurant. No problem, he'd visit Nonna and then he'd— He had no clue what to do.

He ran his hand through his hair. He supposed he could help at the cellar door but his sisters would either moan he was in the way or organise him and neither scenario appealed. He could play tennis but his nieces wouldn't be home to partner him until four. The prickling unease he always experienced in Bandarra had, over the last few days, formed into a tight burr that had embedded itself hard and fast. Too many memories made it impossible to relax and he felt like a caged lion, pacing back and forth.

Talk to Abbie.

He rejected the thought immediately. There were plenty of things he wanted to do with Abbie but talking wasn't one of them. As he crossed the car park he heard a whirring sound and a peloton of cyclists in bright green, white and red Bandarra hospital jerseys shot past him with a wave, and he recognised the physiotherapist and the radiologist. Lunchtime cycling? There was a thought. He'd buy a bike and go riding. A long hard ride in the summer heat was just what he needed to keep the Bandarra demons at bay and to banish a pair of fine green eyes that saw too much.

CHAPTER SIX

ABBIE checked the liquid display on the ear thermometer. 'Mate, you've got a fever, that's for sure.' She gently palpated the boy's glands. All up. 'Have you vomited?'

Alec sniffed and rubbed his watery eyes. 'I chucked after breakfast and now my throat hurts a bit but I'll be OK. Mum needs me to go to the shops. The baby's making her tired.'

Abbie bit her lip. Usually getting information out of an eleven-year-old was like pulling teeth and in most situations with children this age the mother of the child hovered, answering any questions before the child could open his or her mouth. She glanced over at Penny, Alec's pregnant mum, who sat staring out of the window with blank eyes.

When had Alec realised he was the carer in this relationship? She remembered at ten having to make toasted cheese sandwiches for dinner and trying to get her mother to eat. This sort of parent-child role reversal was all too common at the refuge and it ripped at her heart every single time.

She'd called into the refuge just to confirm numbers for tonight's canoeing but Rebecca, the case worker, was out. Another resident had called her aside, voicing her concern for Alec. Penny had silently agreed to the examination with barely a glance when Abbie had knocked on the door of their room.

'Sorry, Alec, but you've got a virus and you won't be going to the shops today or for a few days.' She poured a dose of cherry-flavoured paracetamol syrup. 'You drink this and I'll talk to your mum.'

Alec frowned as if he wanted to object but Abbie put one hand on the boy's shoulder and gave a firm nod. 'You need to get better and then you can help your mum, OK?'

The flushed and feverish child drank the antipyretic, relief burning on his face as hot as the fever. Then he curled up against the pillows and closed his eyes, his body needing the restorative balm of sleep.

Abbie opened her prescription pad and scrawled down an order for an antiviral influenza drug. If

Alec had been at home in a settled environment she would have gone the recommended route for a flu-like virus and advised fluids, bed rest and paracetamol. But Alec's life was far from settled and living in a communal house changed all the rules. She walked over to Penny and gently touched her shoulder. Her palm met fiery-hot skin.

Penny flinched at the touch.

Abbie silently cursed at her uncharacteristic lapse. Too many women who came to the refuge associated touch with pain. 'Penny, do you have a fever too?'

Baby-blue eyes glazed with a pyretic stare turned towards her. Dusky black shadows marked her pale face and bright red fever spots burned on her cheeks. She coughed—a shuddering wet sound—and immediately brought her arm close to her ribs in a guarding action.

Abbie's diagnostic radar went on full alert. 'How long have you had pain when you cough?'

Penny shrugged. 'I dunno. Since Adam hit me.'

Abbie's stomach clenched as memories threatened her. She gave herself a shake and refocused on the woman in front of her. Alec had said they'd lived in Victoria until two days ago. 'Did you see Justin and have an X-ray?'

The mother shook her head as her hand caressed her belly. 'X-rays aren't good for the baby.'

'Neither are broken ribs good for you.' But Abbie was equally worried about the cough and the fever. Put together they meant pneumonia. Pregnancy and pneumonia were a shocking combination, especially in someone so emotionally and physically drained as Penny. Not to mention that they were in the middle of an H1N1 virus pandemic.

Abbie kicked herself. She'd been so focused on Alec when she'd first arrived that she'd associated Penny's blank look with depression but now she was seeing the real picture. 'Can I please examine you?'

Penny shrugged again and Abbie took that as a 'yes'.

Gently lifting her blouse, Abbie stifled a gasp at the purple and yellow bruises on the woman's thin body. There was every chance she had bruised or fractured ribs, which would account for the guarding. Abbie mentally crossed her fingers that the cough was nothing too severe but Warrior Abbie did a massive eye-roll and mouthed, *Get real.*

'I'm going to listen to your chest. Can you please breathe in and out when I say?' Slowly she moved her stethoscope around her patient's back as she listened to the lung sounds. The stark sound of fine crackles in the lower lobes was unmistakable. She tapped the area, hearing the dull percussion sounds. Penny had double pneumonia and probable rib fractures.

'Penny, given Alec's symptoms and your fever and cough, I need you both to come to hospital.'

The sick woman could hardly focus on Abbie. 'It's just a cough.'

'No, Penny, it's more than a cough.' She recognised the malaise of depression and illness where any effort was just too hard. She bent down so she was at eye-level. 'I need to take care of you so you can take care of Alec and the baby.'

Penny stared and then slowly nodded. 'OK.' But she remained seated.

'I'll arrange everything and be back in a few minutes.' Abbie picked up her medical bag and walked out of the house to her car. She didn't need anyone to overhear her phone conversations and panic. She punched in a familiar number.

'Paul Jenkins.' The commanding voice of the senior paramedic answered her call.

'Paul, it's Abbie. I need an ambulance at seventeen Creamery Lane and I'll be here when your officers arrive.'

'No problem, Abbie. We're on our way.'

The call terminated and she rang Rebecca, leaving a message on her service asking her to return to the refuge as soon as possible. Then she scrolled down her contact list and, finding the unfamiliar number she needed, she pressed 'call'. The ringtone sounded long and loud in her ear. 'Come on, come on, pick up.' She paced up and down, the tough buffalo grass of the nature strip springing under her feet. She was about to cut the call when the ringing stopped.

'Leo...Costa.'

The whooshing and rushing sound of exhaled air swept down the phone. Instantly, the image of his broad chest with muscles rippling surfaced in her mind and liquid heat poured through her. She gripped the phone too hard. What was he doing?

Stop it. She didn't want to know. Well, she did want to know but now wasn't the time to be thinking about anything except work. 'Leo, it's Abbie.'

'I'll meet you…in EMD in…ten minutes.' His words, although gasped out, carried one hundred per cent professionalism without a trace of the flirting banter that had tinged their more recent conversations.

Not that she'd seen him since he'd left Theatre after Lorenzo Galbardi's surgery but the fact that he seemed to know instinctively that she needed him for patients gave her supportive reassurance. 'Thanks, Leo, but it's a bit more complicated than that.'

'Where are you?'

'Creamery Lane.'

'That runs parallel with Dorcas Street, right?'

'Yes.' The buffeting noise of wind crackled down the line, making it hard to hear and she didn't want to talk directions. 'Listen, I've got a mother and son with flu and therefore suspected H1N1 virus.'

'How…sick?'

Again with the panting. Was he jogging? The trees waved gently in the breeze, which was completely out of sync with the roaring sound coming down the phone. 'One patient is pregnant and has bilateral consolidation of the lower lobes of the lungs.'

'Hell, that's not good. Do we have a bed in ICU?'

The words sounded clearer and confusingly in stereo. She twirled around to see Leo swinging off a shiny black and red road bike, the hands-free device of his phone still in his ear.

Her jaw dropped of its own accord and she openly gaped as rafts of shivering delight shot through her before pooling deeply inside her and heating into simmering need. He stood before her, his taut, fit body clad in the distinctive green, white and red cycling Lycra leaving very little to the imagination. Every sinew, tendon and ligament was delineated by the clinging material like the chiselled detail on a Michelangelo sculpture.

She fought for a coherent sentence and cleared her throat. 'You're training for the Giro d'Italia?'

He gave her a long, lazy grin. 'Maybe the Murray to Moyne. The Allied Health blokes want to take on Mildura hospital this year so I thought I might join them. This is my first training ride and I was around the corner when you called.'

He removed his helmet and his smile flattened out, with deep lines bracketing his mouth. 'So we hospitalise the pregnant woman and we home quarantine the boy. How is that complicated?'

His no-nonsense surgeon's tone immediately centred her, thankfully banishing every inappropriate sensation. 'The complication is this house is a women's refuge and there are five other women with their children living here at the moment.'

'Can we hospitalise the boy too?'

'Yes, we can but—' She ran a statement through her head, practising how to introduce the tricky topic.

He stared at her, deep lines creasing his forehead and then realisation dawned in his eyes. 'I'm male.'

Oh, yeah, all male. Every single gorgeous millimetre.

He rubbed his hand through his hair, raising glossy jet-black spikes. 'So what's the best way to play it? Do you think the pregnant woman will let me look after her in hospital if I have Erin with me the whole time? That leaves you to examine the rest of the women here at the house and organise education and possible quarantine.'

Surprise fizzed in her stomach. *He gets it.* She

clenched her hands to keep them firmly by her sides instead of letting them fly around his neck in a hug of thanks. So often her male colleagues were offended by the fact that in this type of situation their gender immediately put them at a disadvantage as the refuge preferred a female doctor. But Leo didn't appear to be at all threatened by this. Damn it, once again he'd broken out of the charm-use-and-abuse-box she so desperately wanted him to stay in.

'Thanks, Leo.'

He shrugged as if he was confused as to why he needed her thanks.

'Abbie, Abbie, come quick!' A pale and feverish Alec came running out of the house. 'Mum's fallen over and she's not waking up.'

Abbie ran, hearing the clatter of Leo's cycling shoes close behind her. She found Penny on the floor by the chair she'd been sitting on and with Leo's help rolled her into coma position. She checked her airway and then slid in the plastic airway guard Leo handed her which would prevent Penny's tongue from rolling back. Then she counted her respirations while Leo's long fingers located Penny's carotid pulse.

He pulled his hand away. 'She's tachypnoeic.'

'And tachycardic. I'll insert an IV.' Abbie pulled an IV set out of her bag and rummaged around until her fingers felt the tourniquet. She didn't need to voice her fears that swine flu and pregnancy were a potentially life-threatening combination—she could see that very thought reflected back at her in Leo's inky eyes.

'Will she be all right?' Alec's scared voice broke over them.

Leo stayed bent down and turned so his face was at Alec's eye level. 'Your mum's very sick but Abbie and I are both doctors and we're doing our absolute best to take care of her.'

'And the baby?'

Leo hesitated for half a beat. 'And the baby.'

'Are you sure you're a doctor? You don't look like one.' Alec sounded extremely suspicious.

Leo didn't even blink at the accusatory tone. 'I'm on holiday and I was having a bike ride when Abbie phoned me. Most of the time I wear a suit or baggy green pants and a matching top when I'm in the operating theatre.'

The boy blanched. 'Does Mum need an operation?'

Leo shook his head. 'No, mate, but she needs antibiotics and she needs to be in hospital.'

'I was looking after her.' The words came out on a wail.

Leo gave him a man-to-man squeeze of the shoulder. 'And you've done a great job but now it's time to let us look after you and Mum.'

'Why is her mouth purple?'

Abbie opened her mouth to explain but Leo continued to talk to Alec in an honest and open way without any sign of condescension that some adults used with kids. She begrudgingly conceded it was great stuff for a guy who usually dealt with patients that were asleep.

'Her lungs have got fluid in them and that makes it harder to breathe. See this?' He held up a clear oxygen mask. 'This will help her breathe and in a few minutes you, me and your mum are going for a ride in an ambulance to the hospital.'

The boy's eyes momentarily widened against his fear. 'Really? Awesome.'

Abbie glanced up and, for the first time since meeting Alec, she glimpsed the child that he was. Too often the child got lost in the emotional maelstrom of their parents' chaotic lives. She'd lived that scenario. She taped the IV in place as the ambulance officers arrived.

'Perfect timing, guys. We need her connected

up to the Lifepak.' Leo accepted the ECG dots from Paul and immediately attached them to the unconscious woman's chest.

A moment later the ECG display traced across the screen along with Penny's rapid pulse rate, diminishing oxygen saturation and rising blood pressure. Leo spoke sharply. 'We need to leave now.'

'Oh, God, what happened?' Rebecca, the case worker, rushed into the room, her face white with shock.

Leo exchanged a look with Abbie that said, *You go sort that out; I've got this under control.*

Abbie rose, relief surging through her that she had Leo working with her today. Penny was in good hands and she was going to need every ounce of medical skill they had. 'Paul, Alec and Leo are going back with you.'

The paramedic readied Penny to be loaded onto the stretcher. 'No worries, Abbie. We'll look after everyone.'

She caught Rebecca by the arm, shepherded her out of the room and answered the unasked questions that clung to her face. 'Penny and Alec have flu-like symptoms and, given that we're in the grip of a swine-flu epidemic, we're pretty certain that's what they've got.'

Bec's hand flew to her throat. 'Oh, no. I heard that's really bad for pregnant women.'

Abbie grimaced. 'Penny's extremely ill and we might need to evacuate her to Melbourne if her condition deteriorates any further. I'm also worried about the other residents so I need you to contact everyone and get them back here so I can examine them.'

Bec nodded. 'OK. Most of them went on a picnic but they're due back because of the canoeing, which I guess you'll be cancelling?'

'Postponing, at any rate.' She smiled a half smile. 'Let's have a quick cup of tea and a biscuit and I'll brief you so you can answer the residents' questions. Then we'll turn one of the bedrooms into a clinic and get to work. We're going to be flat out for a couple of hours at least.'

She heard the siren of the ambulance fading into the distance. Leo would be flat out working too.

Leo squinted into the glare of the early evening summer sun and watched the air-ambulance helicopter lift off, the down-draught of the blades swirling the red outback dust into the air. It had been a hellish three hours—every second testing all of his medical knowledge. As a surgeon he was at the top of his field but surgery wasn't what Penny needed.

Murphy, who'd been pressed up against his legs, barked as a familiar white four-wheel-drive turned into the car park and came to an abrupt stop. Abbie jumped out of the vehicle and ran over, her curls bouncing and the wind whipping her plain T-shirt close against her chest.

Leo groaned as his body immediately reacted to her perfectly outlined breasts and perky nipples. The woman was a fashion disaster but if she thought those clothes hid her delicious curves then she was living in la-la land.

'Is that Penny?' Abbie yelled the words over the roar of the engine.

The helicopter banked and headed south, the noise decreasing.

He plunged his hands into the pockets of his white coat, the lapping waters of despair threatening to spill over. 'Yeah.'

'Oh, hell.' Abbie caught his gaze, her mild expletive underplaying the anguish on her face.

The same anguish that filled him. 'Erin and I

did everything we could but she didn't regain consciousness. Her breathing became increasingly laboured and we were worried she'd arrest, so we ventilated her.' He ran his hand through his hair. 'God, I haven't done that since I was a resident. She didn't need a surgeon; she needed a respiratory physician and an obstetrician.'

Abbie shook her head sharply. 'She needed a doctor and she was lucky to have you. Did you consult using the Virtual Trauma and Critical Care Service?'

Her hand touched his arm, her skin warm against his own and her assurance floated through him. 'It was odd talking to my colleagues in Melbourne on a screen but thank goodness for broadband technology. With her pregnancy and the risk of multi-system organ failure, Penny's best chance is in their level one ICU.'

Abbie bit her lip. 'And the baby?'

A familiar hot pain burned under his ribs at his powerlessness in the situation. 'She'd started having contractions so we administered Nifedipine but at twenty-six weeks you know as well as I do that it'll be touch and go.'

Abbie's sigh visibly trembled through her body. 'Poor Alec.'

He automatically slung his arm around her shoulder in a gesture of support. 'Alec's doing well. He's got an IV in, he's rehydrating and his nausea's under control. We'll monitor him but I think after twenty-four hours of Tamiflu he'll be a different kid.'

'But his world is already upside down and now his mother is fighting for her life.' The doctor had vanished. Instead, a hurting woman stood in front of him with the vestiges of a child clinging to her like cobwebs. The familiar shadows that sometimes haunted her eyes had scudded neatly back into place like the dark clouds that heralded bad weather. Then her shoulders sagged and her head swayed, until it finally lost the battle to stay upright and her forehead brushed his shoulder.

An overwhelming surge of protection unlike anything he'd known in years exploded inside him and his hand reached to touch her soft curls. A touch devoid of lust and totally removed from desire. He only wanted to reassure her, murmur into her ear that things would be OK, but most of all he wanted to send those shadows scattering. But this was real life and none of those things were possible. Instead, he held her tight and lowered his face into her hair, breathing in her strawberry scent, soaking up her softness, her spirit and her strength.

Murphy's wet nose nuzzled between them, followed by a bark of, *Hey, what about me?*

Abbie stepped back and Leo dropped his hand, still struggling with the unexpected mix of emotions and glad that Abbie was distracted with her dog rather than turning her all-seeing gaze onto him.

She put her hand on Murphy's head. 'Hey, boy. It's OK; Leo's not all bad.' Then she raised her questioning green eyes to Leo. 'Why is Murphy here?'

He confessed, 'I borrowed him.'

'Why?'

'I thought Alec could use a friend.'

A slow smile wove across her smattering of freckles, lighting up her face, and then she started to move her head from side to side in a disbelieving yet resigned way. 'And let me guess? You called Jennifer Danforth in paediatrics *cara*, produced a box of Baci Italian chocolate kisses, told her that you knew she'd understand that, given the circumstances, Alec needed a buddy and then she let you bring a dog into her pristine ward.'

What the—? He tried hard not to look as

stunned as he felt. How could she possibly have known? Yet Abbie had just outlined in perfect detail exactly what he'd done to get Murphy past Demon Danforth. He shrugged and grinned. 'Hey, it worked.'

Her forefinger shot into his chest. 'Well, you owe me, Casanova. I've been trying to get a companion dog into the hospital for months and that woman has blocked it on every turn.'

He gave her a smug look. 'Did you try chocolate?'

She raised one brow. 'No, but without a sex-change operation and fluency in Italian, I doubt that one would have worked for me.' Her finger jabbed him hard in the sternum. 'So, before you leave, I want an approved companion pet programme policy with Jennifer's signature on it.'

He gave her a mock salute and a wink. 'Yes, ma'am.'

'Good.' But her sergeant major voice had faded to a warm and friendly tone and she dropped her hand to her pager. 'Everything's quiet at the moment so does Murphy have time for a "W" before he has to report for duty?'

The dog's golden-brown eyes moved back and forth between the two of them saying, *I recog-*

nise euphemisms, you fools, and his tail started wagging enthusiastically.

He fondled the dog's ears. 'Sure.'

She hesitated and then cleared her throat before asking, 'Do you want to come too? It's been a hellish afternoon and we could exercise and debrief at the same time.'

The completely unexpected invitation made him smile. 'That's probably a good idea.'

'Great. Let's go, then.' She turned to cross the car park, Murphy pulling on the lead as he headed towards the river path.

The river path. Leo's muscles tensed and his hand shot to his chin. Every part of him screamed to stay put. But he'd already refused the canoeing and if he refused this walk after he'd already committed to it, he knew Abbie would start asking questions. Questions he didn't want to answer.

He made a fast decision. He'd go on the walk and he'd ask questions to keep hers at bay. With every ounce of determination that had got him into medical school and had pushed him up the gruelling surgical career ladder, he fell into step beside her, resolving to find out why an eleven-year-old boy's plight had brought the shadows back into her eyes when other patients had not.

The walking path was as popular and as crowded as the river. Houseboats chugged along overtaken by water-skiers criss-crossing behind speedboats. The high-pitched 'toot' of the horn of a paddle steamer could be heard in the distance, a far more pleasant sound than the buzz of the closer and louder jet-ski. On the path, tourists walked with their families, locals with or without dogs strolled and a gaggle of giggling teenage girls eyed a group of teenage boys. Everyone was out just as they were in Italy for *passeggiata* and catching the cool breeze off the river on a hot summer evening.

The first part of the walk was spent nodding and smiling to people as they passed, commenting on the weather, chatting about dogs, until they got beyond the main part of town where the path narrowed and the bush thickened.

A flash of memory—mallee scrub, dark water and ancient trees—flickered unfocused in his mind and he steeled himself to keep the image sealed away. He felt Abbie's gaze on him and he dug deep, forcing the muscles of his mouth to lift in a smile. 'Remind me never to come along here if I want time to myself.'

'It's pretty popular and why not? It's so pretty.'

She gazed across the brown sparkling water and then licked her lips, the moisture clinging to them making a rosy red.

'Yeah, it's pretty.'

But she missed the real meaning of his words and just smiled at him as a co-conspirator of two people enjoying the view. A view that sliced into him deeply every time he saw it, reminding him of what he'd lost and the trauma that had followed.

She turned back from the river, a genuine smile on her lips that raced straight to her amazingly expressive eyes. 'I know I just gave you a hard time about charming Jennifer Danforth so Murphy could visit the ward, but thanks. It was a lovely idea and you were really great with Alec when Penny collapsed.'

The praise warmed him, pushing the memories away. 'It must be pretty terrifying for him with his mother so ill and I'm gathering his father's out of the picture?'

Abbie tugged on Murphy's lead as he strained forward wanting to chase some little pied cormorants. 'I only met Penny and Alec for the first time today but generally the fact a woman and her child are staying at the refuge means the father's not in the picture.'

He shoved his hands in his pockets, working hard to sound casual as the lapping of the water ate into him. 'Because of violence?'

'Perhaps. Not always. Sometimes women are abandoned or left destitute and they need the support of the refuge to get on their feet again.' This time it was her turn to stare straight ahead and her mouth flattened into a grim line. '*Some* men can be bastards.'

The guttural vitriol in her voice surprised him. Although she'd refused every invitation he'd offered, they'd worked together well and he'd only ever observed respect from her towards Justin and the male paramedics so he didn't have her pegged as a man-hater. And damn it, but the kiss they'd shared made a mockery out of that thought. She'd melted into his arms and kissed him with the expertise of a woman who knew what she wanted out of a kiss and how to get it. 'Perhaps you're getting a skewed view from working at the refuge.'

'Hah!'

The harsh sound echoed back on the breeze and Leo heard the pain. Pain and shadows.

Her voice rose, agitation clearly edging the words. 'You saw the bruising on Penny's chest and you heard how Alec behaved more like he was the parent than the child. That poor kid has needed to grow up way too fast under a roof of uncertainty.'

The shadows in her eyes darkened as she gripped Murphy's lead hard, her knuckles turning white. 'Some men treat women and children like chattels instead of people, disposing of them when they've had enough. They destroy women's lives and leave kids in terrible situations, putting them at risk of it happening all over again.'

The trembling pain in her voice was unmistakable and again he wanted to hold her tight but he instinctively knew that would be the wrong thing to do. What he did know was this reaction was no longer about Alec—it was all about her. He'd bet money on it that it was connected in some way to why she mostly tried to hold herself aloof from him.

'Who left you, Abbie?'

CHAPTER SEVEN

ABBIE'S breath stalled in her throat as Warrior Abbie, who'd been caught napping, frantically pulled on her armour and tried to get her act together. *Who left you, Abbie?* His words hailed down on her with unerring accuracy. How did he know? How had he worked out that everything that had happened this afternoon had brought back in horrifying waves the painful memories of her time with Greg and the insecurity of her childhood?

Still, just because that had happened was no reason to talk about it. If she'd learned anything it was that it was best to just 'get on' with things. She tilted her chin skyward and pursed her lips. 'We're talking about Penny and Alec, and refuge clients in general, not me.'

Mensa-bright eyes looked sceptical. 'Except there's something about their situation that's got to you.'

Denial shot to her lips as her heart thundered hard against her ribs. 'No, it hasn't.'

'I think it has. You're pretty upset and it might help to talk about it.'

Guileless care and concern sat on his handsome face, tempting her to spill her guts and yet terrifying her at the same time. 'I'm so not having a heart-to-heart with *you*.'

'Why not?' He smiled a warm and friendly captivating smile. 'I've been told I'm a very good listener.'

'I'm sure you have.' The moment the cheap shot left her mouth she regretted it.

His jaw tightened, pulling the edges of his mouth downward. 'Abbie, if that comment's to do with me dating a lot of women then let's get something straight—I'm always honest and up front with them. I'm after fun and good times and I never make a promise I can't keep. So don't confuse me with badly behaved men.'

His clear dark gaze seared her as his honesty and integrity circled him, making a mockery of her determination to cast him in the same light as her father. As Greg. She bit her lip, realising she'd just been grossly unfair. Taking out her hurt on him was unwarranted. He was only trying to be a supportive colleague and, hell, she'd been the one who had said, *Let's debrief.* She clearly hadn't thought *that one* through.

She let Murphy lead her down onto a sandy beach. It continued to surprise her that there was golden sand like this so far inland but she wasn't complaining. Murphy barked and she released him from the lead, watching him tear off into the shallows, ever hopeful of catching an ibis. She turned and, with a start, she realised Leo hadn't followed her. He remained standing on the higher bank, his hand rubbing the scar on his chin—something she'd seen him do on and off since she'd met him and usually when he was tense. Damn, but she'd really hurt his feelings.

She trudged back towards him and stood looking up at him, catching his gaze. She'd expected to see anger but it wasn't there. Instead, a mix of undecipherable emotions seemed to be tumbling over each other with no clear delineation but she caught pain. She called out, 'I'm sorry. You're right; today hasn't been easy.'

He held her gaze for a moment longer and a part of her ached. Then, like sunlight breaking through clouds, his eyes cleared and in three strides he was by her side and she was left wondering if she'd imagined the whole thing.

'I shouldn't have lashed out at you; it's just there's too much of my story in Alec's and Penny's and I hate it when I see that it's still happening.' She sat down on the sand and leaned back against a fallen red-gum bough.

Leo lowered himself down next to her in a stiff and uncoordinated way before finally stretching his legs out in front of him.

Funny how all his movements were usually so fluid and he could glide out of a hammock but he couldn't lower himself onto the sand without looking as if all his limbs were overly long.

'Do you and Alec share a father leaving?'

He was far too perceptive and, as much as she wanted to stay silent on the entire topic, she knew she'd lost the battle to keep her story to herself. She'd already had to apologise and if they were to continue to work together as a cohesive team she needed to tell him, otherwise it would hang around like an elephant in the room, affecting their working relationship.

Her palm dug into the sand and then she raised her hand, letting the tiny particles run through her fingers as her mind released her memories.

'My father was a charming but controlling man and he dropped in and out of my life. My mother finally left him when I was ten but the legacy of him never left us.'

A restrained kind of tension lined Leo's shoulders but his expression was one of sympathy duelling with interest. 'How much of it do you remember?'

She stared straight ahead. 'I remember the fear. I remember the routine my mother had before he came home every night, a sort of ritual. She believed if she followed it to the letter it would mean the evening would be pleasant. She'd make dinner and I'd set the table. Then she'd go to her room, reapply her make-up, change into a pretty dress and insist on brushing my hair. After that we'd wait.'

'Wait for what?' Two lines furrowed down at the bridge of his nose.

We have to look pretty for Daddy so he loves us. She tugged at her now short hair as the memory of the plastic brush snagging through her long hair made her scalp prickle. 'We'd wait for my father. On a good night he'd barrel through the door, twirl me around and call me his princess. He'd compliment my mother's cooking and after dinner he'd crank up the music, grab my mother around her waist and they'd dance through the house.'

'And on a bad night?' Leo's hand spilled sand close to hers.

She glanced at him, expecting to see the prying look that people got when they heard a story so at odds with their preconceived ideas of who she was and where she'd come from, but the only thing she saw was understanding. 'A storm cloud would enter the house and we'd be on high alert cyclone watch, just like Port Headland was last week. Will it hit or will it blow past and miss us? It was terrifying even when he didn't hit us because the fear was always there.'

'I can't even imagine what that would be like.' He spoke quietly. 'We're Italian and, believe me, my parents can yell and argue with the best of them, but there was never any fear in the house.' His eyes lit up with a memory. 'Usually Anna did something crazy which distracted them and it blew over very quickly. Did you have a brother or sister to share this with?'

She shook her head. 'Just me.'

'Sorry.' His fingers skated across the back of

her hand in the lightest caress before falling back to the sand.

Heat roared through her and self-loathing filled her. His touch was one of understanding and friendship. Only she could put a sexual tinge on it and, heaven help her, hadn't she learned any-thing from her life? From Greg? She blew out a breath and fixed her gaze on the peeling bark of a tree on the opposite bank and forced the words to keep coming.

'One night he hit Mum so badly he fractured her ribs. The next day when I was at school a taxi arrived with Mum in it. She'd packed one bag for the both of us and we went into supported accom-modation.'

Her eyes burned from staring at the tree but she didn't dare look at Leo. She didn't want to see pity in his eyes—she'd seen that too often over the years from too many people, which was why she kept her story buried deep.

'And you took care of your mother. Just like Alec was doing today.'

She gave a silent nod, letting his deep voice wash over her with its startling insight. She turned towards him, suddenly needing to see his face. Not a trace of pity marked his cheeks,

only admiration and respect. *He gets it.* The realisation jolted her and Warrior Abbie laid down
her shield, although her fingers stayed close to it.
The tightness in her chest slowly slackened and
an unexpected peace rolled through her, seeping
into places that hadn't experienced calm in a long
time. Yet again, Abbie had just glimpsed another
side to Leo Costa. He confused her so much with
his multi-facets, making her question what she
believed, but most of all it made her wonder why
was he hiding behind all that superficial charm
when there was so much more to him.

'So did things settle down for you and your
mother?'

She shrugged. 'Not really. We got out of the
refuge and got set up again. Mum got a job and
had a few boyfriends who always seemed to arrive
with presents and leave us with debt. I craved sta-
bility but, by sixteen, I realised Mum wasn't able
to give me that. I knew then I had to find it for
myself and make a life so I was never dependent
on anyone ever again. I got a scholarship to uni-
versity and studied medicine. People always need
doctors, right?' She smiled, trying to lighten the
mood. She'd had enough talking about herself.

Leo watched her eyes and tried to read them.

His own childhood had been carefree in compari-
son to hers and at that precise moment he totally
understood her self-containment. Anyone who'd
lived a roller coaster childhood of over-indul-
gence followed by abandonment would be very
wary of people. Of men.

But she kissed you. The memory of their kiss
hadn't dimmed at all. It stayed so strong and
clear inside him—a kiss that told the story of an
incredibly sensual woman, someone who'd had
some experience. The women he most enjoyed
being with were totally independent and relation-
ship-free but still staked their claim for a healthy
sex life. But in the last few days he'd dropped
enough hints to Abbie that he was open to some
fun and good times that there was no way she
could have missed them. Nothing he had said or
done had lowered her major 'road block' signs;
in fact she'd done everything she possibly could
do to shut him out. And it wasn't because she
wasn't attracted to him—tangible lust close to
the point of combustion burned between them at
every meeting and, had their kiss been anywhere
else, sex would have followed.

Lust is just a nuisance that can be controlled.

So I was never dependent on anyone ever again.

Her sweet voice replayed in his head and it was like someone switching on a lamp and illuminating a dark corner. Right then he knew exactly what he had to ask. 'And have you been?'

She glanced up from the sand, confusion creasing her brow into a row of deep lines. 'Been what?'

'Dependent on anyone again?'

She rolled her plump lips inward and a shudder ricocheted across her shoulders, down her torso and into the sand. Without thinking, his fingers moved to slide between hers, needing to give her some support, needing to feel connected to her in some way.

She pulled her hand away and fisted it into her lap. 'Let me put it this way; I had the usual casual and fun uni flings everyone has in the first and second year before they grow up. Then I had a relationship that ran off the rails at six months. But it was well after that I had one serious lapse in judgement which cured me for life.'

I hate what you've done to me. Memories of Christina bubbled up inside him and he spoke before thinking. 'Don't be too hard on yourself. I had one of those.'

Her head jerked up. 'I can't imagine you being dependent on anyone.'

Her accurate words whipped him. She was right; he'd never been dependent on anyone but people had been dependent on him. Dom. Christina. He'd failed them both. 'I meant a relationship that cured me for life. I got married at nineteen.'

Her eyes shot open so wide it was like looking into a tropical pool. 'You…I…you're divorced?'

Regret at telling her clawed him because it opened him up to questions like why he'd married his brother's girlfriend. Questions he didn't want to answer. 'Yep.'

Her astonishment slowly faded, replaced with a knowing look. 'I bet Maria wasn't happy about that.'

The corner of his mouth jerked and he took the segue with open arms. 'That would be the understatement of the century, but we all make mistakes.'

She nodded in agreement. 'Oh, yeah, and Greg was my ultimate. I'd got through the gruelling years, I'd qualified and was working in Adelaide.'

Relief flooded him. He'd managed to divert her. 'Financially and emotionally independent?'

'For a short time, yes. I think I'd been working so hard since third year that I'd forgotten how to have fun. When I finally raised my head up to look around at the world, there was Greg, a silver-tongued actor who told me what I wanted to hear.'

For some unknown reason, Leo really wanted to reassure her. 'We're all susceptible to that.'

'Yeah?' Sceptical green eyes flashed at him. 'Well, given how I'd seen all my security disappear again and again as a kid, I should have known better but I stupidly fell hard for the cliché of the happy-ever-after dream. He moved in, I chose china patterns. We shopped and nested and I was the happiest I'd ever been in my life.'

'So what happened?' Half of him wanted to know; the other half didn't want her to relive what he knew would be painful.

'Piece by tiny piece over two years and under the guise of love, he dismantled my independence and, dear God, I let him.' Her ragged sigh reverberated between them. 'After what "the experts" would call the "honeymoon period" his charm started fading and the insidious controlling behaviour came out. He needed me to be with him when I wasn't at work, he didn't pass on messages, he chose my clothes, and he decided where we went and who we visited. Every time I started to question this he'd revert to the man I'd first met and convince me I was over-tired from working too hard, that after a good night's sleep I'd understand I was being unreasonable. He had me second-guessing myself to the point of going crazy.'

'*Bastardo*.' Pure white anger surged through Leo.

She mustered a small wry smile. 'Exactly. The day he hit me I told him to leave. I went to work and when I came home that night the apartment was empty. Utterly empty. He'd taken everything, including the mothballs in the linen press.'

'He took your clothes?' Leo wanted to commit murder. How could someone do that to a person?

She nodded and her shoulders straightened with what he was starting to recognise as her trademark strength. 'Everything. Thankfully, I had work and slowly I paid off my debts and the moment I finished my GP training I came up here.'

'Good for you. New start?'

'Totally.'

'And since then?'

Her brow creased. 'And since then, what?'

'Have you had another go? Tried a healthy re-lationship?'

She shook her head. 'God, no. I choose the wrong men so I'm leaving all that for the people who know how to do it and do it well.'

'Fair enough.' He could understand that line of thinking because he had no intention of ever again entering the black pit of despair that was a long-term relationship. 'What about dating?'

'Nope, nothing.'

'Nothing at all?' He couldn't keep the incre-dulity out of his voice. An amazingly sensual woman sat calmly telling him she was actively avoiding any sort of liaison. It was just plain wrong.

Her lips twitched. 'It's not a tragedy, Leo. I'm happily single and I plan to stay that way.'

Lust is just a nuisance that can be controlled.

'*Dio mio!* Yes, it is a tragedy. I'm happily single too but I'm here to tell you that it doesn't mean you have to lock down every sexual emotion that you have.'

Her mouth tightened. 'Don't be over-dramatic. What's important here is that it's my choice and it works for me.'

He didn't believe that for a minute. 'Really? A lifetime of no sex works for you?'

Everything inside her stilled. *Get out now!* Like the terrifying spray of wild-fire burning embers, his words scorched and burned into her. Warrior Abbie grabbed her shield and ran for a bolt-hole. Abbie stood up abruptly, determined to end this conversation right now. 'Murphy, here, boy.'

The wet and soggy Border collie shot straight to her, shaking sand everywhere.

Leo brought his arms up to protect his face from the sand and then shot to his feet, his eyes blazing with a mixture of pity and desire. 'If we'd been somewhere more private when we'd kissed you know we would have ended up having sex.'

She knew that too but no way was she going to admit it. With shaking hands she reattached the dog's lead and gave Leo her best disdainful glare. 'In your dreams, mate.'

'Oh, but it is.' His usually smooth voice cracked slightly as he stepped in close. 'You can't deny this incredible thing that boils between us every time we're together.'

Her mouth dried. 'I can and I will.' *I have to so I stay safe.*

'Abbie, neither of us is looking for a relationship and we're both very clear on that.' He tilted his head forward so his forehead touched hers. His aroma of mint and citrus overlaid with an all-masculine scent stormed her nostrils. Her heart pounded fast, driving hot blood through her veins, sending her nipples into tight buds of anticipation and pooling moisture between her trembling legs. Every part of her wanted him so badly she thought she'd explode from the bliss.

But she clenched her fists against every tempting sensation and desperately tried to block him out.

He slowly lifted his head and stared down into her eyes, his expression deadly serious. 'Please know that I'm not any of the men who've marched through your life demanding your love with controlling conditions.'

And on one level she really did know that but it didn't stop the fear about herself from battering her.

His expression morphed from serious to a wicked gleam. 'Abbie, remember those casual flings at uni? The ones you told me were fun?'

Panic fluttered so fast in her chest she thought she'd faint. Dear God, he'd really listened to her. Warrior Abbie stamped her foot. *How could you have been so dumb to say something like that to him?*

His voice rumbled around her, warm and enticing. 'We have four weeks where we could have a lot of fun and some amazing sex, enjoy it all and then say goodbye. Use me to banish that bastard's memory with some fun.' His finger trailed down her cheek. 'The invitation's on the table and the RSVP is up to you. Think about it.'

He stepped back, gave Murphy a scratch behind the ears and with four long strides he reached the bank, jumped up onto the path and walked away.

Abbie's legs gave way and she sat down hard on the sand with Murphy licking her face, his expression confused. Bright spots danced in front of her eyes and her body tried to get some blood back to her brain but all her pleasure centres refused to give it up. She steeled her mind to close down every single sensation. Greg's charisma had been her downfall. The day she'd kicked him out, Abbie had gathered her emotions, reclaimed her heart, jammed the lot into a padlocked box and thrown away the key. Warrior Abbie had stood guard over the box ever since—an easy job as there'd never been a single attempt to pick the lock. Until Leo.

Leo, who, when you navigated past the superficial charm, had more facets to him than a radiant-cut diamond. Confusing and contradictory sides, sides that whispered to her that he was a good guy, an honourable man. Whispers she wanted to trust. Whispers that terrified her.

Remember those casual flings at uni? We have four weeks where we could have a lot of fun and some amazing sex, enjoy it all and then say goodbye.

Tingling sensations ripped through her, shaking her to her very marrow and tempting her so strongly she felt weak all over. She blew out a long slow breath. Forget the facets, it was time to regroup. She mentally ran over her 'life is good' list. She had a good job, lovely friends, a dog who adored her and she was safe. She'd spent years working to keep safe, making sure she kept safe.

Use me to banish that bastard's memory with some fun.

Nothing about Leo was safe.

And so help her; that was the one thing that called so strongly to her and threatened her the most.

'*Dottore*, you need sleep.'

Abbie sat sharing lunch with Maria. She hated to admit it, but she was also hiding from Leo. He'd already visited Maria so she knew she was safe. Maria was right, she needed sleep, but sleep had refused to need her last night. She'd tried watching TV, reading, a long warm soak in the bath, yoga, deep breathing and relaxation but nothing had kept her mind from constantly re-hearing Leo's invitation. *Fun, amazing sex, good times and then goodbye.*

Every time those words rolled over in her head, images of rolling over with Leo wrapped around her had followed, leaving her skittish and completely wound up. Could she really have an affair and keep safe? Could she pretend she was eighteen again and have fun? The thought kept taunting her, calling her and driving her insane.

'You're right, Maria, I need sleep but yesterday was a difficult day.'

'My grandson, he no sleep either.' The old

woman put her work-worn hand over Abbie's.
'This woman and her baby, they are sick, yes?'

'Very sick.' Leo had met her at the clinic this
morning with the news that Penny's baby had
been stillborn and Penny was in multi-organ failure, fighting for her life. Murphy was spending
the day with Alec.

Maria grunted. 'A crazy world this is when an
old woman lives and the young they die.' She
tapped her finger imperiously on the table. 'I want
to go home for the vintage.'

Abbie sighed, knowing that when Maria made
up her mind it was hard to dissuade her of anything but the family had agreed that Abbie was
the doctor in charge and that Maria was only to
be discharged when Abbie considered it appropriate. Maria's walking was improving each day
but it was still a bit too early for her to go home.
'When's the vintage?'

'When the grapes are ready.'

'Yes, but what date is that?'

Maria rolled her eyes. 'When the sugar is right.
Could be tomorrow, could be next week, could
be longer, but I must be home for the twenty-
seventh.'

Abbie calculated how many days until the specified date, wondering why Rosa and Anna hadn't mentioned its significance to her if Maria was going to get so het up about it. 'Is that a special day?'

Rheumy eyes usually so full of gritty determination suddenly filled with a resigned sadness and an unusual melancholy circled her shoulders. 'It is a day not to forget.'

Abbie tried not to frown at the cryptic answer. 'Well, if you keep working hard on the physio and the occupational therapist can install the necessary rails and bars in time, then there's a chance you could be home for the twenty-seventh.'

'I *will* be home.'

Abbie leaned forward. 'Maria, I can't make a precise promise but I can discuss it with your family and Leo—'

Maria's fist came down on the table, her eyes glinting as stormy black as her grandson's. 'Leo knows why and he has to be there too.'

A shiver ran down Abbie's spine, leaving behind a sense of unease. *Don't be a drama queen; you just need a good night's sleep.* But one thing she did know—nothing she could say would stop Maria from being where she had to be on that date. But why did Leo need to be there too?

CHAPTER EIGHT

'ABBIE, got a minute?'

Leo's deep velvet voice washed over her, immediately sending her tightly wound body into an overdrive of delicious tingling sensations. Her hand clenched hard against the pencil in her fingers, almost breaking it in half, but still the streaks of unfulfilled need burned hot inside her, tugging at every hard-held resolution. Warrior Abbie lay weak and wounded as the invaders yelled, *Just say yes, get naked and get him out of your system. Have some no-strings fun; how dangerous can it be?*

For two days she'd only seen Leo at work and he hadn't made any attempt to bring up the neither accepted nor declined invitation that lay between them. He'd surprised her again. The fact that he'd really meant that the RSVP was completely up to her and strings-free should have given her some relief, but just thinking about him sent her body into meltdown and her brain into a tailspin.

'Sure.' She carefully put her pencil down, willing her hand not to shake, and she glanced up. Leo and a woman, equally as dark and attractive as him, stood on the other side of the nurses' station. His wide smile raced to his eyes as he slung his arm around the woman's shoulders with the air of a man in very familiar territory.

A bright green flash streaked through her, spiralling around all her good intentions and shocking her to her toes. *No, no, no.* She couldn't possibly be jealous because she didn't care enough. The flash morphed into a face and thumbed its nose at her.

'Abbie, I'd like to introduce you to my sister, Chiara.'

Sister. Abbie hated the relief that settled through her as she stood up and walked around the station. 'Pleased to meet you, Chiara. Leo didn't mention he had more than one sister.'

Chiara extended her hand with a laugh and a smile. 'I think he likes to pretend he only has one but there are three of us.'

'Three bossy, opinionated women.' But Leo didn't sound at all disgruntled and his eyes twinkled like the night star.

Chiara elbowed him. 'Three sisters whose

friends provided you with a limitless supply of dates in high school.'

Abbie laughed. 'Poor Leo; it must have been tough growing up in a household of strong women. I bet you dreamed of having a brother.'

His ready smile vanished, replaced by a grim tightness around his mouth that seemed to whiten the scar on his chin. A sharp pain unexpectedly jabbed Abbie in the chest before dissolving into a dull ache that lingered. She instinctively rubbed her sternum.

Leo cleared his throat. 'Chiara, her husband, Edoardo, and their sons are a registered foster family so I spoke to the social worker and Alec's going to be discharged into their care.'

Surprise at the idea gave way to comforting warmth that wove through Abbie at Leo's thoughtfulness. 'Oh, that's wonderful. What a great idea.'

The woman nodded, understanding clear on her face. 'We live at the vineyard too so, with Anna's girls, my boys plus the other cousins who live on the adjoining property, there're plenty of kids and lots of distractions.' She sighed. 'My heart is sick just thinking about Alec. Leo says his mother is frighteningly ill and fighting for her life.'

Abbie bit her lip and caught Leo's tense gaze. 'I just got an update from Melbourne City and Penny's now on extracorporeal membrane oxygenation.'

'Hell.' His eyes closed for a fraction of a second before opening again, his anguish for Penny's battle mirroring her own.

Chiara turned to Leo, questions clear on her face. 'Is that bad?'

Leo nodded. 'It's the last defence against swine flu. It's a machine where the blood is drawn out of the patient by a pump which acts like a replacement heart, and then it's pumped through this strange diamond-shaped device which adds oxygen into the blood and removes the carbon dioxide before the blood's returned to the patient.'

'So a machine is being her heart and lungs?' Disbelief rang in the words.

'That's right.' Abbie wrung her hands. 'Right now her lungs are so badly affected by the H1N1 virus they can't do their job. We need to hope that she'll recover but it's going to be a long, hard road.'

Chiara rolled her shoulders back. 'We'll look after Alec for her. When can I take him home?'

'In a couple of days.' Abbie and Leo spoke

together, their voices contrasting like a melody. Leo winked at Abbie, his smile now firmly back in place, and her stomach went into free fall.

'Great.' Chiara pressed her bag to her shoulder. 'I'll go and spend a bit of time with him now and then visit again tomorrow with the boys.' She spun on her heel and then turned back. 'Oh, Abbie, I forgot to say but Mamma wanted to invite you to the blessing of the grapes and the vintage picnic. Of course the date's still up in the air but it's getting really close and you've been so great with Nonna that we'd love you to be there.'

Abbie's cheeks burned hot as Leo's penetrative and questioning gaze bored into her over the top of Chiara's head. One that said, *Now, this will be interesting. I dare you to come.*

Leo would be at the picnic and avoiding him would be impossible. But refusing an invitation like this would be social suicide in the small Bandarra community and she had to live here long after Leo had returned to his city life. *Fun, amazing sex and then goodbye,* the whispers taunted. *He will leave and that will keep you safe.*

The words hammered her and she closed them down by focusing on Chiara's expectant face and pushing her mouth into a smile. She hedged her bets. 'As long as there's no emergency, I can be there.'

'Fingers crossed, then.' Chiara smiled.

Her fingers rolled in against her palm. 'Fingers crossed.'

'Ciao.' Chiara presented her cheeks to Leo, who kissed her quickly in a European farewell, and then she walked briskly towards Alec's ward.

Abbie's stomach rumbled, reminding her it was lunchtime, and she headed towards the front entrance of the hospital. Leo fell into step beside her. 'Are you going for a training ride today?'

As they reached the automatic doors he stood back, allowing her to proceed first. 'I thought I—'

'Abbie!'

She pulled her attention from Leo and swung quickly around at the strangled sound of her name.

Morgan Dalhensen ran towards them, dripping wet, clutching an equally wet child against his chest. 'Help me.'

Abbie and Leo sprinted across the car park.

The man stumbled as they reached him and he

almost threw the child into Abbie's arms. 'He's not breathing.'

The child felt as floppy as a rag doll in her arms, and the telltale sign of blue lips had her kneeling immediately and laying the child on the ground. She checked his airway, hoping for something as easy as a physical obstruction that had choked him but knowing the high probability was he had water in his lungs. Her fingers met no obstruction. She checked for a pulse. Nothing. She moved her fingers, trying again.

'One minute he was on the riverbank and the next I couldn't see him and I turned my back for a minute and, oh, God, help him.' The anguished father's voice rained down on her.

'Starting CPR.' Abbie rolled the toddler over and realised Leo was still standing stock still next to her, his gaze hauntingly bleak and empty and fixed fast on the child. She'd expected him to have already run to ED for the emergency resuscitation kit and a trolley. 'Leo.' Her elbow knocked his leg hard. 'Get the resuss kit. Go.'

As she pinched the child's nose and lowered her mouth to make a seal, Leo finally broke into a run. She puffed in two breaths and started compressions, counting out loud with each one.'

'Come on, Zac,' Morgan's voice pleaded into the hot summer air.

Come on, Zac. The sound of running footsteps and the more distant sound of rattling trolley wheels reassured Abbie as she puffed in two more breaths and started the next round of thirty compressions.

A wailing moan filled with distress broke from Morgan's lips.

'We need to get him inside and warm him up.' Leo's voice wavered as he scooped Zac up and put him on the trolley.

Abbie climbed up next to the child, continuing her compressions as Leo and Erin ran the trolley into ED.

The moment they were in the resuscitation room and Abbie's feet were back on the ground, Leo moved in next to her, attaching the boy to the monitor. 'Erin, get him out of his wet clothes and wrap him in a space blanket. We need to warm him up.'

'Doing it now.' Erin deftly cut away the boy's small shorts and T-shirt.

The monitor started beeping and Leo gripped his chin as he stared at the green tracing. 'We've got a heartbeat but he's extremely bradycardic and needs CPR to maintain his circulation.'

Abbie's arms kept compressing Zac's chest to keep his blood moving. 'Leo, intubate him.'

Leo whitened under his golden tan, the scar on his chin almost luminous. 'Your arms will be tired. You tube him and I'll take over compressions. On my count of five.' His voice, usually so firm and sure, creaked over the numbers. 'Three, four, five, change.'

What? Her arms were fine but Abbie didn't question the change because every second counted. She couldn't understand why Leo wanted her to tube the child when they probably both had the same amount of experience in tubing a toddler— virtually none.

Erin wrapped the boy in a space blanket.

Abbie opened up the paediatric laryngoscope and tilted back Zac's head. The tiny light cast a glow and she visualised the vocal cords, which was always a good start.

Erin handed her the small ETT tube.

Holding her breath, Abbie slid the tube carefully along the silver blade of the 'scope, between the tiny cords and into place. She immediately withdrew the scope.

Erin ripped off lengths of tape. 'I'll tape, you suction.'

With fine tubing, Abbie suctioned the ETT tube, clearing some brown-coloured fluid that squirted into the holding container.

'God, his lungs are probably filled with bloody brown river water.' Leo's ragged voice scraped against her like cut glass.

Erin attached the air-viva and connected the oxygen before rhythmically squeezing the bag, forcing air into the child's damp lungs.

Leo's hands looked ludicrously large against the small child's chest. 'He needs atropine to bring up his heart rate.'

Abbie picked up the tourniquet. 'I'm putting in a line.'

Leo nodded curtly, his face full of sharp angles and taut cheeks.

A shiver chilled Abbie. She'd never seen him look so tense or grim, not even in Theatre when Jenny was close to dying under his hands on the operating table. Zac was one sick child but Jenny had been just as ill so his reaction puzzled her.

She snapped the tourniquet onto Zac's tiny arm, her fingers fluttering over his skin, trying to find a vein. Nothing. She moved the tourniquet to his leg and started over. 'He's shut down, I'll have to—'

'Stop stuffing around.' Leo's eyes blazed with fear. 'Just put the damn adrenaline and atropine down the ETT tube, Abbie. Now!'

Erin's large brown eyes widened at Leo's edgy and frantic tone and her hands shook slightly as she prepared to disconnect the air-viva.

Abbie drew up the drugs, the uncharacteristic tension cloaking them like thick fog. What was going on? She'd never seen Leo lose his cool before but right now his normal and easy control of situations was unravelling like a skein of wool.

Erin removed the air-viva and Abbie dispensed the drugs. 'Atropine and adrenaline administered.'

Leo kept compressing Zac's heart and Erin pressed air into his lungs and Abbie stared at the monitor, silently counting. The beeping sound slowly increased as the drugs took effect. Abbie breathed a sigh of relief for Zac. They were winning.

She wanted to high-five but one look at Leo's pinched face had her feeling as if they'd just lost. What was going on with him? He should be as relieved as she was. She smiled at him, willing him to smile back with his trademark grin, the one he used with effortless ease, but his tense jaw and tight mouth stayed in their grim line as he stopped CPR and stepped back now that Zac's heart was pumping fast enough on its own.

She knew Zac wasn't totally out of the woods yet, given he had river-water-induced pulmonary oedema and a massive risk of infection. 'I'll be happier with Zac at the Royal Children's under specialist paediatric care.' She stared straight at Leo, somehow knowing he needed to be out of the room. 'Erin and I have got this covered. Now he's better perfused I'll be able to get the IV in, so you go ring the air ambulance and then bring Morgan back so I can explain everything.'

Leo's dark brows pulled down as if he was about to object but he stayed silent, his face etched with sorrow. His fingers rubbed the scar on his chin before falling away and caressing the child's hair. Wordlessly, he turned and walked out of the room.

Abbie's heart clenched and she had to stifle a gasp. From the moment Leo had laid eyes on Zac he'd changed. It was as if she'd just truly seen the real Leo for the first time. A man stripped bare of his social props and now totally exposed. Everything about him that she'd feared—his charm and charisma—had vanished. Even the things she admired like his care and professional control had taken a beating and all that was left was a hurting and tortured man. The real Leo.

The realisation stunned her. Every barrier she'd erected to keep him at a distance fell to the ground. Right then she knew that, the moment she could, she had to go to him. She had to find him and do whatever it took to help him.

Leo's thighs burned as he powerfully pressed and pulled the pedals of his bike around, each revolution taking him further away from the hospital, further away from the helipad and everything connected with the now-resolved emergency. But the Bandarra demons sat hard and heavy on his shoulders, digging in deep. Christina's screaming voice and Dom's total silence had bored into him from the moment he'd seen Zac, keeping him back in the past when he'd needed to be in the present.

A child had needed his help and he'd totally frozen.

Blinking against the flashes of red soil, green

vines, black road and blue sky, he watched the numbers on the bike computer climb to thirty-five kilometres an hour. He had no destination in mind—he just had to ride. Ride until he could feel nothing and forget everything.

His chest muscles strained as he used every atom of oxygen in the hot torpid air and still he pushed harder, taking himself as close to the edge of what his body could bear. He didn't want comfort; he wanted pain. He drove himself until his body turned inward, completely consumed by the overwhelming physical demands. Until all extraneous thoughts, noises, sounds and scents were blocked from his consciousness.

Ten kilometres later he slowed and the tightness in his chest eased, his leg muscles ceased to burn and relief flowed through him. He opened a water bottle and chugged down half the contents, his body soaking up the fluid like a dry crinkled sponge, and then he poured the rest over himself. Pulling off his helmet, he wiped his brow with his bandana and, as his body gradually uncoiled from its exercise-survival mode, his eyes progressively focused on his surroundings.

The distinctive wiry leaves and furrowed bark of the bull-oak came into view, followed by the blue-green leaves of the river red gums with their peeling bark of green, grey and red. His chest tightened as his head swung around, taking in the muddy edges of brown water, and then his gaze zeroed in on the distinctive carving on one of the trees. *Dom and Christina 4 Eva.*

Wadjera billabong.

His heart pounded hard in his chest, pushing a dull and unrelenting ache into every part of him. Why the hell had he ridden here? A place he'd avoided for years. The ride was supposed to help him forget because he sure as hell didn't want to remember.

Every part of him urged him to leave. Buckling his helmet with numb fingers, he prepared to click his left foot into the pedal before swinging his right leg over the seat and riding away fast. Very fast.

The crackling noise of tyres on gravel made him pause. He turned to see a very familiar white four-wheel drive pull into the clearing. Like a film in slow motion, he heard the engine die, the click of the door opening and saw a pair of shapely legs jump down before the owner appeared from behind the door clutching an enormous basket.

A pair of questioning green eyes hit him like a king-punch.

'Leo.'

'Abbie.' How had she known he was here when he had no clue he would be?

His heart sped up. She'd want to talk about what happened with Zac. Women always wanted to talk. *Get on your bike. Leave now.*

Her sweet scent wafted towards him and part of him hesitated. Every cell in his body urged him to flee and his hands gripped his racing handlebars. *Just keep running.*

'I have to get back.'

She stepped closer and a flicker of disappointment flared against banked heat, followed by something vague, half-formed and undefined. She chewed her lip. 'Really? I thought you could do with some time away from the hospital. I brought food and drink.' She lowered the basket onto the ground.

The pull to leave couldn't stop his gaze from following her every movement. The sway of her hips, the way her no-nonsense navy-blue straight skirt moulded to her pert behind and the fact that her plain T-shirt fell forward when she bent over, exposing creamy mounds of flesh peeking out of pink lace. His groin tightened. *Go anyway.*

He opened his mouth to use his time-honoured excuse that had served him so very well for many years—work. But his words stalled. He wasn't needed at the hospital or the clinic and Abbie knew it. If he used that excuse, the questions he didn't want to answer would start immediately.

She straightened up and stepped in close. His hand released the bike, letting it slip back to rest on the tree. Reaching up, she cupped his cheek with her hand, her smooth palm deliciously cold against his stubbled cheek. She tilted her head back until he was staring deep into luscious pools of rainforest-green that invited him to dive right in. 'I'm here for you, Leo. Please stay.'

He was instantly hard. Her voice caressed him like the cool and welcoming softness of silk trailing against hot skin, and a deep crevice opened up inside him, desperately seeking that softness and urging him to lose himself in it. Offering him another way to escape. He lowered his mouth towards hers, searching for the haven he so desperately needed.

Abbie recognised the moment Leo decided to stay. Recognised the fading of whatever it was that terrorised him and saw the burning lust move in to replace it. Lust that she recognised intimately—hot, burning, driving desire that stole every rational thought and absolutely nothing could slake except raw, primal sex.

'I need you, Abbie.' The tormented and hoarse words filled the space between them as his gaze burned for her.

'I know.'

His lips slid across hers, enticing, demanding and giving. All thought evaporated. She was past thinking, past analysing and way, way past resisting. He needed her and she wanted him. Call it comfort, call it sex. She'd given up resisting him the moment she'd seen his façade crumple. Wrapping her arms tightly around Leo's neck, she didn't care he was sopping wet. Nothing mattered except he was in her arms and his mouth was hard against hers.

She met his kiss with one of her own as every firmly suppressed molecule of longing ripped out of its box, splintering its now flimsy enclosure and exploding inside her in a maelstrom of sheer seeking pleasure. Nothing existed except her driving need for him. She plunged her tongue inside his mouth but nothing had prepared her for the assault of his flavour, filling her so hot and fast that her knees sagged and she fell against him.

Without moving his mouth, Leo instantly clamped one arm against her back, pulling her hard against him. His arousal pressed hard up against her belly, his fingers delved in her hair and his other hand found her breast.

White stars exploded in her head as his thumb caressed her through her T-shirt, her nipples pebbling into hard, sensuous buds straining against the exquisite touch. A moan rose to her lips as she panted against his mouth, frantic to have more of his touch on her and at the same time desperate to touch him.

'Got…to…feel…you.' Leo swung her around until her back rested against the bark of a tree and his hands pulled at her T-shirt, hauling it over her head. With a flick of his fingers, the bra clasp came undone and her breasts thankfully tumbled out of her bra and into his waiting hands. She cried out from the wonder of the skin-on-skin caress.

His hand stalled. 'Too fast?'

'No.' She grabbed his hand and, with a frenzied push, pressed it back on her quivering and heavy breasts. She could hardly speak, she couldn't think at all, she just had a primal drive to feel every part of him on her. She knocked his helmet off his head and tugged at his shirt, splaying her fingers against rock-solid muscle as she traced his spine, vertebrae to vertebrae from his neck all the way down to his hips, memorising every tendon, bone, swell and crevice.

'You're beautiful.' He rasped the words out as he moved his lips from her mouth and up along her jaw. His tongue delicately traced the curve of her ear before his teeth nipped her ear lobe.

Pleasure shock waves rocked through her and she gasped, bucking her hips towards him. She heard a growl and then felt his arms under hers and suddenly her feet left the ground.

'Leo.' It came out on a wail of need. She could only force out one word as her body completely took over. One word to represent all that she wanted. She wrapped her legs around his waist and her chest rose and fell with short shallow breaths. Every part of her yelled to have him and she gripped his upper arms and threw herself back against the tree, totally consumed by her desire to have his mouth against her breast.

His mouth suckled her as his hand slid along the

soft skin of her inner thigh. She gripped his head as whirls of colour swirled and joined like paint on an artist's palette. Then his fingers brushed the damp, silky crotch of her panties.

Exquisite pleasure rocked her.

His thumb traced tiny circles and then pressed firmly but gently against her.

She sobbed as shafts of wonder built to breaking point.

His fingers stilled.

Her fingernails gripped his back. 'No, don't stop.'

With his thumb still pressed against her, he curved a finger around the edge of the silk and slipped it inside her. She shattered and pure bliss poured through her.

But it wasn't enough. Her body now completely ignited, roared for more. Frantic to feel him, her hands shot down his back, fingers clawing against the waistband of his bike shorts as gut-wrenching frustration hit her. She couldn't reach any further.

'You're sure?' His ragged voice breathed against her ear.

'I'm way past sure.'

His arms cupped her buttocks and she rose

slightly for a moment before leaning back. Her hands found their target. Leo shuddered against her before raising her up again.

This time he lowered her gently. Her body screamed for him but it had been a long time and he took it slowly, moving in a little, out a little, which drove her crazy.

'Just do it.'

'Wait.' His growl quivered with hard-held restraint.

She didn't want to wait. She wanted him buried deep inside so he was as close to her as possible. With a cry she pushed down and her muscles almost sobbed in relief as they wrapped themselves tightly around him in a caress they'd ached to give him for so long.

She lost herself in him as they rose together. A scream left her throat as her body flung her into orbit far, far away from him, and as she returned she held him as he shuddered and sagged against her.

A moment later she felt the sharp prickle of bark against her bare back, felt the ripple of a hot breeze against her bare breasts and she gazed down into glittering black eyes. Reality thundered back in brilliant Technicolor. The shadowy image of her mother surfaced. Oh, dear God, what had she just done? She dropped her head into her hands and groaned, 'Well, that was embarrassing.'

Leo gently tugged her hands away from her cheeks. 'No, it wasn't; it was fantastic.'

She shook her head. 'We just had sex in less than four minutes and outside in the open air as if we were animals on heat instead of respectable pillars of the community.'

'Yeah.' He grinned like a kid who'd just got away with stealing lollies. 'I kept telling you what lay between us was explosive. Plus, let's face it—' a wicked grin lit across his face '—you were a ticking time bomb.'

She groaned again and let her head drop onto his shoulder. 'I was so easy.'

His finger caressed her chin and then tilted it upwards so she had to look into his eyes that glowed with desire and appreciation. 'You were amazing and if you're so worried about the frenetic speed, I promise to make long, slow, languid love to you. Just give me a few more minutes.' His grin suddenly faded as if he'd been zapped by electricity. 'We didn't use protection.'

Her voice rose on the back of her agitation.

'That's what I mean. We should have known better; we're doctors!'

He lowered her down so her feet hit the ground and then he bent and picked up her T-shirt. As he handed it to her, frown lines scored his brow and a horror-struck look loomed large in his eyes. 'Hell.' His hand raked his hair. 'OK, well, emergency contraception is eighty per cent effective so the stats are on our side, right?'

She tugged her shirt over her head, stunned that pregnancy was his first concern. 'Leo, it's not pregnancy I'm worried about. I've still got an IUD in from…' She stopped, refusing to think about her past.

The frown faded and he wrapped his arms around her and dropped a kiss into her hair. 'Abbie, stop worrying. You're the only woman I haven't used a condom with and, as you've been celibate, am I right in thinking we're both healthy and there's nothing to worry about?'

His arms urged her to snuggle in against his chest and seek refuge in his reassurance. 'I guess so.'

'So stop worrying.' He trailed kisses along her forehead and down to the bridge of her nose and her blood immediately fired off rafts of tingling and an overwhelming need for him consumed her.

'But if you want long and languid in a bed we need to leave right now.'

Laughing, they grabbed their belongings and ran to the truck.

CHAPTER NINE

ABBIE lay in her bed, propped up on one elbow, while her other arm lay across Leo's chest, her fingers absently tracing along his ribs while her gaze stayed fixed on his face. Part of her couldn't believe she had a man in her bed but Leo had needed her. His pain had called to her so strongly it had hurt, and she didn't regret the sex at all.

His heavy-lidded eyes smiled up at her. 'We're not very good at long and languid yet but I think we could improve if we keep practising.'

She laughed, thinking about the wild, almost uncontrolled coupling in the shower before they'd hit the bed and managed to slow things down slightly. Even so, the sex hadn't been a one-way thing. Since coming home he'd been a generous lover, giving as much back to her as she had offered to him.

Leo wound a curl around his finger and pulled her head down to his. 'If you want, we've got a month to get it right.'

'A month?' Could she do that? It was a period of time with a firm end-date so it came with built-in protection.

He nodded. 'You can make up for lost time and we can have four weeks of fun. You can't deny the sex so far has been amazing.'

And she couldn't deny it. She couldn't deny that her body had craved him from the moment she'd first seen him. She wanted him and she didn't want to fight herself any more. She lowered her mouth, grazing his lips with hers. Her traitorous heart hiccoughed but Warrior Abbie was too busy reclining with a cigarette in her hand to provide any sort of protection. *One month, one month, one month.*

'A month it is, then.' She stared down into black eyes filled with tenderness but she could still glimpse the lingering and lurking shadows. The time had come to find out what had put those shadows so firmly in place.

Leo lay back on the pillow, not able to remember when his body had been this relaxed or content. For days his dreams had been filled with Abbie but the reality of having her in his arms and the explosive sex they'd shared blew the dreams out of the water. Abbie would make these few weeks in Bandarra bearable. Nonna was improving and Abbie was the perfect distraction from everything else. He just had to hold it together for a bit longer and then he could leave Bandarra still in one piece.

Her fingers drew tiny circles across his chest, slowly creeping up his torso, and his breathing slowed as he enjoyed her touch, his mind spinning out on all the ways they could enjoy each other over the next few weeks.

'What's the story behind this one blemish on an otherwise perfect face?' Her forefinger caressed his chin, neatly tracing the outline of the now-white-with-time scar.

His hand shot out, his fingers clenching around hers as his sense of peace vanished and every muscle tensed under the assault of adrenaline. 'No story.'

Knowing green eyes bored into him. 'Then why do you have the same look on your face that you had when you saw Zac?'

His breath jerked in his chest. 'Don't exaggerate. How can you compare me lying here after mind-blowing sex with the life-and-death situation we had this afternoon?'

But, like a dog with a bone, she wouldn't give it

up. 'Leo, I've never seen you lose your cool, even when Jenny almost exsanguinated on the table, but you did today.'

And he knew it. His temples throbbed and he shifted into damage control, using a politician's ploy of diverting a question with a question. 'What? You don't get that extra tug when it's a kid that might die?'

Two deep lines carved into the skin at the bridge of her nose. 'Of course I do but it was more than that with you.'

The jarring sound of a hammer against metal clanged in his head. She was getting too close. 'Just leave it alone.'

Her lips pursed and her brows shot up under a tangle of curls. 'Like you left me alone after Penny and Alec?'

Her words sliced into him, carving straight down to his moral compass. He sat up, swinging his feet over the side of the bed, intending to get up and walk away, not caring that his only clothing option was sweat-soiled cycling gear.

'Stop running, Leo.'

Her voice punched him from behind. 'I'm *not* running.'

'Yeah, you are. Just like you did this afternoon.'

Her hand touched his shoulder and a part of him wanted to throw off her touch but most of him wanted to hold on to it. Hold it tightly. He shrugged his shoulder and spoke through clenched teeth. 'I went on a bike ride, Abbie.'

Her soft palm stayed put. 'With something chasing you. When you left Theatre you looked like you'd seen a ghost and I was so worried about you.'

Building panic dug in. 'Well, you didn't have to. I'm a grown man and I didn't need you chasing after me. Anyway, how did you know where I was?'

'I asked Maria where you might have gone and that's how I found you.'

Fury and betrayal burst inside him as grief pummelled him, and he refused to turn around and look at her. 'Nonna shouldn't have told you anything.'

She blinked in surprise at his tone. 'She didn't say anything other than you might be at the waterhole. But I'm stringing snapshots together, Leo—today with Zac, you walking away from canoeing, your grandmother's need to be home by the twenty-seventh.'

Her words cloaked him and right then he knew he'd just hit the dead-end of a very long road. He slowly turned around to see her sitting cross-legged on the bed, beautiful and serene. Something so strong and kind pulled at him, unlike anything he'd ever experienced from anyone. Two decades of holding everything at bay collapsed around him. He pulled her down and lay with her, his arms tight around her as if he feared she'd disappear, but if he was going to bare his soul he needed her as close as possible. 'You know this morning you said you bet I'd wished I had a brother... Well, I have one. Dom.'

His throat tightened and he forced out the words he hated to say. 'He drowned in front of me when I was nineteen.'

His pain hit Abbie so violently she shuddered for the youth who'd suffered that trauma and for the adult that still held it so close. She rested her forehead on his. 'I can't imagine how awful that must have been.'

'I've pretty much tried to forget.'

'Doesn't work, though, does it?'

His jaw clenched. 'I was doing OK until today.'

She didn't believe him but she let the comment pass, not wanting to interrupt his story.

His arms tightened around her again. 'Growing up, we were inseparable. We shared a room, we rode our bikes everywhere, and the only time we spent apart was at school. I was a year ahead.'

'The twins that weren't?'

He huffed out a breath. 'Something like that, at least right up until I left for uni, anyway.' He buried his face in her hair for a moment and then continued. 'When I came home in the mid-year holidays, we met Christina. She was a cousin of one of the local families and she'd just arrived from Italy for a year in Australia. She was a country girl, pretty naïve and a bit overawed by how different things are here, so my parents insisted we do the right thing and invite her to picnics and introduce her to our friends. We had a lot of laughs and she had a bit of a crush on me but my focus was on uni and I headed back and didn't really give her another thought. By the time I came home for the long summer break, Dom and Christina were very much a couple in the intense way only almost eighteen-year-olds in their first relationships can be.'

Abbie remembered. 'No one else in the world exists?'

He grunted. 'That's right and I got a shock. The last time I'd been home, Christina had been more my friend than Dom's and I guess I expected things at home to stay the same. Not that I loved her more than a friend but it was odd seeing my younger brother with a girlfriend. Dom had always looked up to me, even though I was only a year older than him, and whenever he had a problem he'd talk to me about it. Now Christina was his confidante and my brother didn't seem to need me any more.'

Abbie frowned in concern. 'But he would have.'

His voice became hoarse. 'Yeah, he did, but when he came to me for help I let him down.'

His agony reverberated through her and she held him tightly.

'It was a stinking hot day and we were at the waterhole just before I headed back to uni. After a summer of him avoiding me, it was Dom who suggested we go. We'd been swinging off the old rope we'd put in a giant river red gum years before and talking about all sorts of stuff and I realised how much I'd missed his company. And then he told me Christina was pregnant. He'd knocked up an Italian girl whose traditional family wouldn't take her back unless she was married.'

Abbie could picture two teenage youths, not quite men, trying to deal with one of life's biggest dilemmas. 'That would have been pretty scary.'

Leo's eyes burned with unbearable memories. 'I was so furious with him for putting himself in this position where he had no choice, and stalling his life before it had even started, that I yelled at him. I called him a jerk, a moron and plenty of other unspeakable things. He yelled back and told me if he'd wanted to hear crap like that he would have told Papa. He stormed off towards the water, preparing to bomb into it and shut me out.'

His words slowed and he shuddered. 'My rage had me picking up my towel to leave and then Christina arrived. I couldn't speak to her so I strode past her and, as I did, I heard a terrifying crack. Christina screamed and I turned around to see a huge tree limb crash into the billabong, taking Dom down with it. I remember shouting his name, running into the water, diving under, but you can't see a thing in that freaking muddy water. I ripped myself on snags but I kept diving. On the third attempt my hands touched his legs and I pulled but he was wedged tight under the tree. I couldn't move him.' His eyes darkened into bleak black discs. 'I let him down, I let him die.'

Abbie's stomach rolled and acid burned her throat. Shocked by his words, she gripped his arm hard. 'Leo, it was a tragic accident. You didn't let him die. The red gum limb probably killed him before he went under the water.'

He wouldn't meet her gaze. 'Dom was under that tree because I drove him away instead of helping him. I let him die.'

Her palm pressed his cheek, gently pulling his face to meet hers, needing him to understand. 'Leo, I'm sorry the last words you had with your brother were harsh but you know gums just drop limbs without warning in extreme heat. This was bad timing but it wasn't your fault.'

He shrugged, his jaw tense and his cheeks hollow. She knew her words hadn't touched him, hadn't even grazed what he believed and she blinked back the urge to cry.

In an emotionless tone Leo continued. 'He died on February the twenty-seventh and you're right, that's why Nonna wants to be home. She visits the billabong every year on that day.'

The Costas had lost their child, Leo had lost his brother and a young woman had lost her first love. Abbie's thoughts went to her, pregnant and grieving in a foreign country. She did a quick calculation and worked out the baby would now be almost the same age as his father was when he died. 'Does Christina visit?'

He shuddered. 'No. When we got divorced she went back to Italy.'

'*You* married Christina?' Her shocked voice sounded unsteady to her own ears.

A steely rigidity entered his body. 'I had to. I had to make it right. Dom would have married her and because of me he died. I took her to Melbourne and married her quietly there. She miscarried soon after and I lost the last part of Dom I had.'

She could hardly take it all in. Duty, honour and heart-wrenching pain lay deeply hidden inside this complex man.

'And what about you?' Abbie asked the question but she had a strong idea she already knew the answer.

He ploughed his hand through his hair. 'I haven't

been back to the waterhole since the accident. At least not until today and God knows why I went—I sure as hell wasn't planning to. Hell, I hardly visit Bandarra unless I have to. This trip is the longest I've stayed in years.'

'Perhaps it was time.'

He gave her a look that seared her. 'I didn't take you for a New Age guru.'

He was picking a fight but she refused to give him one. She'd seen past the image he wanted the world to see—the successful surgeon and charming man. She now knew how much it was costing him to stay in Bandarra, to spend time with his beloved grandmother. With his family. With the memories that plagued him.

She realised with startling clarity why he'd pursued her so relentlessly. Why he'd been as desperate as her this afternoon out at the billabong. Why they'd literally self-combusted with need, but for very different reasons.

Her heart cramped and she crossly ignored it. So what that he wanted to use her to forget. She was using him for fun, sex, good times and then goodbye.

You had sex with him because you saw a hurting man who needed you.

She slammed the voice out of her head. No. She had sex with him so she could get this bubbling desire out of her system and then find her even keel again. The one that had served her well for three years. Neither of them wanted a relationship. They could both use each other for a month and then walk away. Safe in that knowledge, she gently pushed him onto his back, slid her body over his and kissed him.

'Good wines are made in the vineyard and nothing can be rushed. A bit like life, eh?'

Leo felt his father's hand grip his shoulder and knew the part of his father who was the backyard philosopher had finally caught up with him. They were walking through the vines with the rich irrigated soil sticking to their feet. Stefano had caught Leo alone in the house and had insisted he inspect the grapes with him.

'So how is your life, Leo? It's been a long time that you've been on your own. I think you're too much like the winery right now—busy holding your breath.'

The last few weeks before harvest was like a long-held breath. A breath of hoping and waiting. Hoping the weather would conspire to provide ideal conditions for the fruit to flourish to perfection. Waiting for the moment the grapes reached idyllic ripeness. Once that happened, the winery inhaled like a long-distance sprinter ramping up for the final assault, embracing the fast pace that the harvest dictated. The harvest took weeks because the moment one varietal of grape was harvested and crushed, another variety would ripen and the process would start again. But right now the winery held its breath.

Leo shrugged and tried not to feel ruffled by his father's question. 'Papà, my life is fine and filled with work and friends.'

'And beautiful women who fill your bed but not your soul.'

Stunned, Leo stared at his father. Not since his divorce from Christina had his father ever passed comment on his personal life and, as Leo lived in Melbourne, it was easy to hide the parade of women who marched through his life. 'I'm happy, OK. I'm a respected surgeon at the top of my profession and that's enough for me.' But his voice sounded overly defensive and the need to silence his father shot through him. 'Most parents would be proud of that.'

'Being proud is not the issue.' His father's mouth

flattened into disapproval. 'You might just be surprised at what you find if you looked at women
with your heart instead of your mi—'

'Papà!' He stopped his father, knowing full well
what he was about to say. 'I'm thirty-five, not—'
The chime of his phone interrupted him. 'I have
to take this.'

'Of course you do.' Stefano nodded sagely and
walked away.

Leo barked down the phone as irritation and
exasperation with his father churned inside him.
'Leo Costa.'

'Oh, you sound like that scary Mr Costa, the
surgeon. I was after the Leo Costa who enjoys
kicking back over a complex red wine, loves a
really good argument about the pros and cons
of federal funding for the state's public hospital
system, and who might just be up for a night-
time picnic in the moonlight out by Cameron's
junction?'

The sound of Abbie's voice instantly drained
away his frustration. The last few weeks had been
amazing. They'd argued long and hard about all
sorts of things, ranging from politics and town-
planning to films and books, and she'd challenged
him on just about everything. Half the time he

wasn't certain if she really disagreed with him or if she was just taking the contrary view to stir him up, but either way he thrived on the intellectual stimulation. And then there was the sex.

'A picnic?' Knowing her appalling lack of culinary talents, he teased her. 'What's on the menu?'

'Me.'

Her husky voice had him hard in a heartbeat. 'I'm on my way.'

Abbie smiled. She'd been smiling a lot over the last few weeks. Spontaneous grinning was probably a more apt description. Work filled her days but Leo filled her nights. He was an inventive and considerate lover and the sex was amazing but, as much as she craved his body, she craved his mind. He made her laugh until her sides ached and tears poured down her cheeks. He argued passionately for what he believed in and, even if their ideas didn't coincide, he didn't freeze her out or put her down. That was a completely new experience and it frequently disconcerted her.

'*Dottore*, you are happy today. This is good. Like Leo, you need to smile more.' Maria sat in her chair, her hand on her stick and her suitcase by her side.

Abbie laughed as she signed and wrote 'February twenty-sixth' on the discharge papers, which were clipped to the chart. 'Maria, Leo smiles all the time, especially at pretty women.'

The grandmother tilted her head and gave her a hard stare. 'But it is not the smile of real happiness.'

The old woman's insight slugged her but, before Abbie could form a reply, Maria was on her feet. 'So I beat the calendar, yes, and today I go home.'

'You're one determined woman, Maria, but don't get too tired or you risk falling.'

'Pfft.' Maria kept walking, heading towards the exit. 'I will sit when I need to. And you—' she pointed a gnarled finger at Abbie '—I will see you in my kitchen soon.'

A flushed and running Rosa met them at the entrance, her car parked under the canopy. 'We'll do our best to make sure she takes it easy.' She opened the car door and settled Maria into the front seat before closing the door and turning back to Abbie. 'Sorry I'm late, but finally Stefano has declared the vintage starts tonight in the cool of the evening. Leo did tell you, we'd very much like it if you could come to La Bella for the pre-vintage picnic and blessing of the grapes.'

'I'd love to, Rosa, thank you.' For the last week or so Abbie had experienced this niggling urge to see Leo in the heart of his family. She'd tried to ignore it because the idea was just crazy. They'd agreed to casual and fun, nothing more and nothing less. But he sprinkled his conversations with stories of his sisters, and being an only child made her want to experience—even if only vicariously—family life.

The older woman smiled and squeezed her hand. 'We're thanking you for all you've done for Nonna and for putting up with Leo's antics when he first arrived.' She sighed. 'He finds it hard to be home.'

Abbie bit her lip and made a split-second decision. 'Especially at this time of year. He told me about Dom.'

Rosa closed her eyes for a moment and then opened them, her gaze clear. 'My boy was in the wrong place at the wrong time and I miss the man he would have been.' Her face clouded. 'Each year I light a candle and give thanks for the vintage that keeps us all busy.'

Abbie wasn't sure keeping busy was helping Leo. 'I think Leo blames himself.'

Rosa's mouth flattened and her words became clipped. 'He is the only one who does.' She jangled her keys and rounded the car. 'I'll see you tonight.'

Abbie waved absently, deep in thought.

Abbie pulled into the vineyard and both she and Murphy jumped down from the four-wheel drive. Kids were charging around, kicking a soccer ball, and right in the middle of the melee was Leo, holding a squealing five-year-old girl on his shoulders and taking a shot at the ball.

He'd make a great father. She bit her lip hard to jolt away the errant and unwanted thought. Connecting Leo with children was madness. He'd been totally up front about what he wanted and so had she. The plan didn't involve anything beyond a few weeks.

Murphy barked. Alec emerged from the pack and ran towards the dog. Leo turned, a long, slow, potent smile weaving across his face.

A tingle of desire shot through her, draining her brain of every coherent thought, just like it did every time she saw him.

'Abbie, can Murphy come and play soccer too?'

She pulled her concentration back and saw that Alec had his hand buried in the dog's thick black and white coat. Three days ago Leo and Chiara had flown Alec to Melbourne for a day to see Penny, who remained in ICU but was now thankfully breathing on her own. She had a long road of recovery ahead of her and, as soon as she was more stable, she'd be transferred to Bandarra, which would be much better for Alec. Since the trip, he'd lost the pinched and worried look that had understandably tagged him as he dealt with the fact that his mother was desperately ill.

Abbie smiled at him, knowing how much he loved the dog and how much Murphy was helping him get through all the upheaval in his life. 'Sure, but he'll probably just want to charge around the outside trying to round you all up.'

'That's OK.' Alec ran back to the game with Murphy bounding after him.

Leo jogged over, the little girl still on his shoulders, giggling joyfully. 'Giddy up, horsey.' The child slapped her hand against Leo's dark hair.

'*Cara*, this horse needs a break.' He lowered the girl down. 'Adriana, this is my friend, Abbie.'

The little girl yelled, 'Hello,' and then raced back towards the soccer game.

Leo grinned. 'So much energy.'

Abbie laughed. 'You poor old thing.'

'Hey, who are you calling old?' He snaked his arm around her waist and pulled her close, his lips grazing her cheek. 'You're looking gorgeous.'

I expect you to dress well, Abbie, because what you wear reflects on me. She tried to shut down Greg's voice, but still unwanted embarrassment knocked against years of not caring how she dressed. She dressed for herself these days and never for a man. Being with Leo didn't change that but, despite knowing it, her hand moved on its own accord, brushing the red dust from her khaki shorts.

She tilted her chin, a combination of crossness at herself and defiance on the rise. 'So I'm a bit untidy but I got held up at the Aboriginal clinic. I'm sorry I missed the blessing of the grapes but if I'd changed I would have been even later.'

A light frown creased his brow and concern flickered in his eyes as he stroked a curl behind her ear. 'Abbie, I'm not being facetious; you look just like you always do, which is beautiful.'

She searched his voice for a hint of hypocrisy,

for the tinge of emotional blackmail she associated with Greg, but all she could hear was sincerity. Her heart rolled over. *No, no, no.* She breathed out a long slow breath, determined to let the compliment wash over her without leaving a mark, but just as the final caress was receding, part of her hooked into it, holding it tight, like an addict clutching at their drug of choice. *Don't be so weak; you don't need any man's approval.*

'Come on, let's eat.' Leo grabbed her hand and they followed the sound of a concertina, laughing and chattering voices. Italian and English intermingled seamlessly, floating on the warm air and creating a sound full of joy and anticipation.

Excitement at being part of this event bubbled in Abbie's stomach. She walked through the gate into a large courtyard bordered by the smoky grey-green foliage of olive trees which were strung with tiny white bud-lights. Between the trees, citronella flares burned, giving off their pleasant aroma and keeping the mosquitoes away, and a large sail overhead cast much-needed shade from the low evening sun. About fifty people crowded into the area, all dressed in heavy-duty work clothes. Abbie felt right at home.

'Dottore, buona sera, com sta?' Maria envel-

oped her in an out-of-character hug and kissed both her cheeks.

'*Grazie, va bene.*' Abbie's tongue clumsily wound its way around the Italian response of 'good, thanks,' much to the amused laughter of Maria, who kissed her a second time.

Leo's parents greeted her warmly, as did his sisters and brothers-in-law, as well as many other people she barely knew. Her own family had been so tiny, she was almost overwhelmed by the enthusiastic greetings and she found herself gripping Leo's hand overly hard.

Leo was kissed by everyone, and with remarkable good nature he accepted his sisters' teasing, unsolicited opinions and instructions until they breached his tolerance. He silenced them with a gruff, 'Abbie's been flat out all day and needs food.'

It was like the parting of the Red Sea. They fell back, full of apologies, and urged her forward to eat.

'Sorry about that; they mean well, but...' His voice trailed off for a moment before he swept an arm out. 'So what takes your fancy?'

Five long tables groaned with more food than Abbie had ever seen in her life. The centrepiece of each table was a large bunch of plump green grapes—the reason for the gathering—but they fought hard for space with huge platters of salami, prosciutto and mortadella which sat beside Maria's delicious bread.

Bowls of glossy black marinated olives, fire-engine-red sundried tomatoes and roasted capsicum and eggplant all called to be stuffed into bread. Dazzling green asparagus nestled with egg and fine slices of parmesan and that was just the first table. Salads of tomato, basil and red onion tangoed with balsamic vinegar, deep bowls of peppery rocket waited to be matched with freshly cooked yabbies, and tangy pesto dip harmonised perfectly with a large dish of schnitzels.

'What's inside those simmering pots?'

'*Bolognese.*' His black eyes twinkled as he gave her a wink. 'You didn't think we could feast without pasta?'

She smiled up at him. 'What about pizza? I'm still dreaming about that *quattro formaggi* that Sofia made for us.'

His voice dropped low and stroked her like velvet. 'I'm still dreaming about what happened afterwards.'

Her cheeks burned at the memory and Leo

roared laughing. '*Tesoro*, don't even think of being embarrassed. You're an incredibly sexual woman so be proud of that.'

Proud? She felt her brows pull down and she glanced at him for the second time in a short period to see if he was being ironic but the sincerity in his voice and eyes was unmistakable. She urged her heart to stay aloof from this complex man who didn't often behave the way she expected, but it rolled anyway, adding to the mix of confusion and uncertainty that churned inside her. Frantic to change the topic, she asked for a drink.

His expression turned serious. 'I'm sorry, but wine and pizza are served at the post-harvest picnic when the grapes are all in. This meal is really for the workers—a sign of our faith in them to bring in the crop quickly and carefully so the grapes are in perfect condition for Papà to turn them into more prize-winning wine.'

Abbie shook her head in bewilderment. 'Wow. It's hard to believe that this isn't a party.'

'This is work but wait until you come to the launch of the latest sauvignon blanc; now *that's* a party.'

His easy inclusion of her in his family's plans

caught her by surprise and added to her already
see-sawing emotions. Weren't affairs hidden
away? Kept private? They'd agreed to a month
together and yet here she was in the heart of his
family, with Leo standing next to her, his arm
slung easily around her shoulders and pulling her
in close, as if she belonged.

Don't even go there.

'Hey, Uncle Leo!'

A group of girls led by identical twins headed
straight towards them and Abbie, needing some
space to round up her wayward daydreams,
slipped away and let the group surround him.
She piled a plate high with food, filled a glass
with refreshing *limonata* and sat down to eat, her
eyes never far from Leo.

From what she could work out, he'd organised
the girls into groups and appeared to be setting up
some sort of game. Whatever it was, he had their
complete attention and cooperation. The relaxed
expression on his face was apparent through his
entire body and there was no sign of any resentment that the kids had ambushed him and interrupted him. She thought about how he'd gone out
of his way for Alec and she realised with a jolt
that he was a man who genuinely liked kids.

So what; it changes nothing. And it didn't. She'd given up on her dreams of motherhood when she'd realised she couldn't trust her judgement in men and no child should have the instability she'd had. As much as she knew she could make arrangements to have a child on her own, she hadn't quite been able to work through the chestnut that her child would never know his or her father. She ripped open the bread roll and shoved in roasted capsicums and eggplant. So what if Leo was great with kids? Why had her mind even gone there? He was adamant he didn't want any permanency in relationships so that meant he didn't want children and neither did she.

The increasingly niggling questions about his marriage to Christina reared their heads again and she tried to bat them away but they stayed, demanding answers.

Anna slid into a chair next to her and tilted her head towards her brother. 'King of the kids is my big brother. It's a shame he doesn't have any of his own.'

Abbie sipped her lemon drink. 'Everyone makes their own life choices. Marriage and family doesn't suit everyone.'

'It works when you choose the right partner.'

Anna's keen gaze zeroed in on Abbie. 'He's been remarkably relaxed these last few weeks.'

Abbie knew dangerous territory when she saw it so she bit into her crusty bread but Anna kept her speculative stare firmly on her. 'Perhaps he just needed a holiday.'

Anna laughed. 'Is that what you're both calling it?' But her face immediately sobered. 'Abbie, I love Leo with all my heart but ever since his divorce he's run from commitment like it was the plague. Please be careful.'

Abbie squeezed the woman's arm. 'Anna, there's nothing to be careful of. Leo and I are having fun, nothing more and nothing less.' But as every hour she spent with Leo ticked by it was harder and harder to convince herself that fun was all it was.

The huge white lights lit up the vineyard like a night match at the Melbourne Cricket Ground and the grape pickers moved along the rows like locusts. Leo finished his row and turned to see Abbie, the tip of her tongue peeking out between her lips in concentration as she snipped bunches of grapes from the vine.

Her eyes shone brightly and her curls seemed

even wilder than usual in the cool air of the night. God, he loved her hair. He loved its sweet scent, the silky way it stroked his skin when they had sex, and the sense of peace that filled him when he buried his face in it. He couldn't get enough of Abbie and usually at eleven o'clock at night he was wrapped around her in her bed, forcing himself to leave her so he didn't have to face a million questions from Anna in the morning if he missed breakfast.

He walked up behind Abbie, plucked the secateurs from her hand and dropped his face into her hair, resisting the urge to tell her how gorgeous she was. Unlike most women, compliments seemed to make her edgy, which was probably a legacy from that controlling bastard, Greg. A legacy he wished he could wipe away. 'I've fulfilled the tradition of each family member harvesting a row.'

She turned in his arms. 'I have a new respect for fruit pickers. It's really hard work.'

'So is being a doctor, so come on, we've got to be at work in eight hours.'

'Thank goodness; my shoulders are killing me.'

He stared down at her and smiled. 'I'll give you a massage before you go to sleep.'

Abbie tried unsuccessfully to stifle a yawn. 'Ah, sleep, what a glorious thought.'

Disproportionate disappointment rammed him.

She laughed and kissed him. 'Don't ever play cards, Leo; you'll lose.'

She pressed in close to him as they walked the two-kilometre distance back to the house. The further away they got from the bright lights, the more the Milky Way appeared, a carpet of stars twinkling high above them in the clear, dark sky. 'I had no idea picking grapes at night meant less splitting and a lower risk of oxidation.'

He loved the enthusiasm she had for all sorts of things. 'What else did you learn tonight?'

'That Anna knows we're having sex.'

He stopped short and slapped his hand against his forehead, knowing exactly what his sister was like. 'What did she say to you?'

Abbie's mouth quirked up at the corners. 'Nothing to panic about. It wasn't anything I didn't already know. She just said that since your divorce you were a commitment-phobe.' She looked up at him. 'Does your family know why you married Christina?'

His gut tightened and he realised with a shock

that Abbie was the first person he'd ever told the truth about his marriage. 'They thought I was trying to hold on to Dom and if they had their suspicions about a child they didn't ask and they were too numb with grief to question anything. They weren't happy but what could they do; we were adults in law.' He bit his lip. 'I never told them about the baby—they had enough to deal with.'

Abbie's arm tightened around his waist. 'You did an incredibly selfless thing.' *Misguided but selfless.*

He pulled away as the memories roared back. '*No*, I didn't. All I ended up doing was hurting the woman my brother loved and doing a pretty good job on damaging her life as well. We'd had the expectation of a baby, something that was part of Dom, and then we were left with nothing.' He started walking, needing to move. 'She was distraught and needy and wanted to try for another baby. I was struggling to study and working to keep us solvent and a child wasn't something I could deal with right then. I buried myself in study and work and she took solace in medication until one night she took too much. After they'd pumped her stomach she asked me for a divorce.

She told me the shame of returning to her village as a divorcée was better than the living hell of being married to me. I thought marrying her was the right thing to do but all I did was drive her mad and exacerbate her grief.'

Sadness loomed large in Abbie's eyes and her hand touched his arm, her fingers gripping him. 'I'm sorry. I doubt you made her depression worse. It would have been hard for both of you.'

He stopped walking and dropped his face into her hair, needing to breathe in her soothing scent and trying to push away the part of his life he usually kept under control. 'All I know is that no relationship is worth the hurt and when kids are involved it's even worse.'

She leaned back slightly, a small frown line forming across the bridge of her nose. 'But what about now? Do you regret not having kids of your own?'

The tightness in his gut unexpectedly extended to his chest and his words shot out overly loud and defensive. 'I've got a heap of nieces and nephews.'

She patted his arm. 'That's what I told Anna.'

She understands. The insight rocked through him, seeping into places untouched for so long by any hint of a real connection with someone. No one in his family understood why he hadn't remarried or had children, especially his sisters. Women usually wanted babies and the thought snagged him. 'What about you, though? Most women I meet want to have children.'

She stiffened against him and her tension ringed him. 'I'm not most women, Leo, you know that.' A tremble ran through her voice. 'I don't want to have a child on my own and with my track record I don't trust myself enough to choose the type of man who'd value me and a child more than himself.'

A finger of sadness crept through him at how much Greg had scarred her, despite him understanding her choice.

A joyous bark pierced the night air and Murphy bounded to the gate as they reached the home paddock garden. Her body slackened against his and she laughed. 'Besides, I've got Murphy and I'm involved with kids at work and at the shelter so I get plenty of kid time. Just like you get with your nieces and nephews when you visit.' She rose up on her tiptoes and kissed him, her eyes filled with the simmering glow he recognised so well. 'All care and no responsibility, right?'

'Absolutely. All care and no responsibility.' He grinned down at her, loving that she thought along the same lines as him. Sex, fun and good times. Meeting Abbie had been the saving grace of being back in Bandarra. Leaning forward, he returned her kiss, melding his mouth to hers and completely ignoring the ache that throbbed under his ribs.

CHAPTER TEN

THE beeping of the alarm slowly penetrated through the many layers of Abbie's deep and peaceful sleep. Consciousness came at a leisurely pace—her body, cocooned in warmth and comfort, was not willing to give up its slumberous tranquillity easily and it held out until the vague and annoying noise became harsh and incessant.

Leo's chest was spooned into her back and his arm curled around her with his hand gently cupping a breast. A very tender breast which ached from the light touch. She moved his hand slightly.

He groaned as the beeping continued. 'Turn the damn thing off.'

Now fully awake, she reached out and shut off the noise as a shower of delight rushed through her. Leo had stayed the whole night for the first time, having declared that if Anna knew they were sleeping together there was no point in pretending otherwise and turning up for breakfast.

Abbie rolled over and stretched her arms above her head, feeling renewed and energised in a way that only restful sleep could deliver. She hadn't slept like that in— Her brain stalled. She couldn't even remember. She kissed him on the nose. 'We have to get up.'

One black eye opened and glared at her before closing again.

She ran a finger down his spine. 'I gather you're not a morning person.'

He raised himself on an elbow and gave her a wide smile. 'I think you'll agree I do my best work at night.'

She wriggled her nose. 'Well, I can't possibly agree with that statement until I have all the numbers, and morning statistics are definitely lacking.'

An imaginative glint streaked through his eyes. 'I love a challenge.'

She kissed him and then pushed at his shoulders. 'Take it on notice then, Mr Costa, because it's Wednesday. You've got a full Theatre list this morning.'

He ran his hand through his thick hair with the

remnants of sleep still lingering around his eyes. 'A full list? I usually do half days.'

'Don't ask me; you were the one who suggested it at our first planning meeting and you need to get going because the visiting anaesthetist from Melbourne gets grumpy if he misses his evening flight back to Melbourne.'

A look of disgust crossed his face. 'People need to pull their heads out of their closeted world. The days of not being able to get decent food outside of Melbourne are long gone. We should delay him and take him to Anna's restaurant, which is equal to anything in Melbourne.'

Surprise slugged her and a tiny seed of hope unexpectedly sprouted. She didn't even bother to quash it. 'Sounds like you're reconnecting with Bandarra?'

He shrugged. 'I just choose not to visit very often but that doesn't make me disconnected.'

But she knew that was a lie. Bandarra had too many ghosts for him. *It's Wednesday.* The words crashed into her brain like an out-of-control semi-trailer and she froze. Wednesday the twenty-seventh. The anniversary of his brother's death. Suddenly the reason for his full list become stunningly clear—he planned to ignore the anniversary, just as he'd always done.

Frustration and concern tumbled in her gut. Leo needed to grieve for his brother in a healthy way so he could see that he wasn't responsible for his death and that his misguided atonement hadn't been the sole reason for Christina's depression.

Leave it alone; don't get involved. Warrior Abbie snapped her book shut with a bang and, for the first time in a long time, concern hovered on her face. Abbie stared her down and extended her hand, demanding her warrior's sword. *He needs me to fight for him.*

He won't want you to; he won't thank you.

I have to. I love him.

She gasped as the last of her protective blinkers crashed to the ground and her heart broke free of the now frayed restraints. Restraints that had been worn away over the last few weeks by the essence of a man who hid his real self from the world.

'You OK?' Care and concern flared in Leo's eyes.

No! Panic doused her, making every muscle twitch and jump. She was as far from OK as she could possibly be but she couldn't let him know that. 'Look at the time!' She threw back the sheets and ran to the bathroom, closing the door behind her. Sinking to the floor, she laid her head in her hands. Bile scalded her throat, her stomach roiled and churned, and despair dumped over her like a towering wave.

She loved Leo.

Her heart spasmed. Dear God, how stupid had she been? From the moment he'd looked into her eyes at the waterhole and told her he needed her, she'd been a goner. She'd been kidding herself ever since. From that moment, along with the picnics, the conversations that went long into the night and meeting his family, her desire for him had only continued to grow but in a totally different way. A bone-deep way that made lust look sad and superficial.

She'd fallen in love with a man who only wanted the superficial. *Stupid, stupid, stupid!*

She dragged in a breath, trying to find calm. Leo was only here for another week and then he would be gone. Nothing had to change with their plan just because she'd broken her side of the bargain. Her heart cramped so hard she caught her breath and then she flinched as her excruciatingly tender breasts touched her knees. She stretched her legs out in front of her, welcoming the coolness of the tiles.

She'd never thought love could be such a physical pain.

'Abbie? Are you sure you're OK? Can I use the shower?'

Leo's voice sounded muffled through the closed door.

Alarm zinged through her. She couldn't let him see her like this because he'd start asking questions. She just needed a few more minutes to pull herself together. 'Use the back bathroom. There are towels and soap all there.'

Hauling herself to her feet, she turned on her own shower, catching the slow-to-warm water in a bucket until the hot finally came through. As she moved the bucket she saw there was no soap in the holder so she bobbed down and opened the vanity. A shampoo bottle fell out of the overcrowded cupboard and she made a mental note to clean out the clutter. As she replaced the shampoo her fingers brushed a box of tampons. A thought snagged her. It seemed a long time since she'd used one. When had she last had a period? Her mind creaked backwards. *Before Leo arrived.*

All her blood drained to her feet and she swayed

as her brain melted. 'I have an IUD.' She muttered the words in an attempt to slow the panic that tore through her. 'They have a ninety-nine per cent success rate. Periods are late when life is different. Breasts are tender when cycles are longer.'

But even when her life had been totally chaotic when she was a teenager and when she'd been strung-out living in the minefield that had been her relationship with Greg, she'd never missed a period. A wave of nausea hit her and she kept muttering, trying to hold on to faltering control. 'Stop it. You're stressed, so of course you feel sick. It's just an association of ideas.' She tried to put a stop to the rising mountain of evidence in her head. She was a doctor, a scientist and she operated on facts, not supposition. An HCG urine test was the only definitive diagnosis and an early morning urine sample the most reliable.

Whipping a towel off the rail, she clumsily tied it around her and dashed into the hall, grabbing her medical bag, and giving thanks that Leo was in the other shower and not able to question her.

She ran back, locking the bathroom door behind her and somehow with trembling hands managed to open the packaging, tearing frantically at the thick plastic cover. Passing urine was the easy part. Waiting the three minutes was an eternity. So she didn't go crazy; she had a shower, dried herself and then closed her eyes and breathed in and out three times. *You're overreacting. It's going to be one blue line.*

She opened her eyes and the stick shot into focus.

Two blue lines.

She put her head over the toilet and vomited.

'Leo, your *nonna* has rung the switchboard every hour this morning; your mother called twice, Anna called and Chiara left a message.' Erin walked into the doctor's lounge waving a sheaf of yellow pieces of paper.

Leo was grabbing a quick bite to eat before he headed back to Theatre. He knew exactly what the messages were about. Nonna wanted him to go with her to the billabong and had sent in the troops as extra backup. He didn't want to speak to any of them. Just because he was in Bandarra today didn't mean he was changing his behaviour. No way was he going out to Wadjera billabong.

You went with Abbie.

An image of Abbie in his arms with her head thrown back against the tree and her eyes wide with the wonder of an orgasm slammed into him and his breath jammed in his throat, causing him to cough.

Go back today with Abbie. The thought circulated, gathering momentum.

He clenched his teeth. *I'm never going back.* Going back wouldn't achieve a thing, and he abruptly extinguished the thought. He'd let his brother down the day he died, he'd let Christina down, and revisiting the scene wouldn't absolve him of that. Instead, he had his day all planned out and his night as well, and all of it added up to work. He might be 'home' but he was an adult and not subject to being told what to do—not by his father, mother or grandmother.

'Is it your birthday?' Erin winked at him as she handed him the messages. 'You better buy us cake if it is.'

He dragged up a smile. 'If I bring in tiramisu tomorrow do you think Helen on the switchboard would ring them all and say I got the messages but I'm tied up in Theatre for the whole day?' It was easier to lie by omission than go into the truth.

Erin laughed. 'For cake and for you, I'm sure that can be arranged. See you in ten.'

She walked out and the visiting anaesthetist looked up from his paper. 'Now that's a change.'

Leo hadn't warmed to his colleague but working harmony deemed he be polite. 'Sorry, I don't follow?'

The other doctor folded the paper in half. 'You have to admit, compared to frumpy McFarlane, that bit of skirt's worth looking at.'

A cold anger chilled Leo to his marrow. 'Abbie McFarlane is a fine doctor.'

'Sure she is, but you have to admit she's nothing to write home about.'

Somehow he managed not to lunge at the self-satisfied bastard's throat. 'Look at her eyes next time you see her and try calling her plain after that.'

'Mate, you surprise me.' He gave Leo a man-to-man leer. 'It's not the window to the soul that interests me about a woman.'

Revulsion filled him. Surely he'd never been that shallow but his father's voice mocked him. *Beautiful women who fill your bed but not your soul.* He downed his coffee. 'We need to get back to it.'

The anaesthetist rose to his feet. 'What the hell were you thinking when you drew up this list?'

Leo managed to grind the words out. 'I like to keep busy.'

'We're going to be here until well after dark,' the anaesthetist grumbled.

'That's the general idea.'

But his colleague didn't hear the muttered words, having already left the room.

Abbie stared into space. Thirty hours had passed since the two blue lines on her pregnancy test had burned into her retinas. Ever since that moment, everything she looked at was framed by those lines. Two uncompromising lines.

Pregnant.

A baby.

Motherhood.

It was the best and worst possible news.

She re-spun the pregnancy wheel and chewed her lip. By her reckoning, she was four weeks pregnant and she'd worked that out so often she'd worn the date off the wheel. Just pregnant but pregnant enough to know her life had irrevocably changed. The doctor in her knew she had to see an obstetrician as soon as possible to have the IUD removed. Those sorts of practical decisions were the easy ones. Telling Leo—that came under the banner of way too hard. He'd already married one woman out of a misguided sense of duty and that was still eating him alive.

I love kids… No relationship is worth the hurt and when kids are involved it's even worse.

She put her head down on her desk and dragged her fingers through her hair. She loved a man who didn't want a relationship or children, and she was pregnant with his child. A man who would feel honour bound to do the right thing, no matter how much he hated the thought. How much more of a disaster could she have possibly plunged herself into?

She sat up and drank a glass of water. She hadn't seen or spoken to Leo since yesterday morning because he'd gone into self-imposed hiding to get through the anniversary of Dom's death. It hadn't surprised her at all when his text had come through saying, *Delayed at work. Tomorrow night, I promise. Leo X.*

Leo, the man she loved. The father of her baby.

Her phone beeped and she read the screen. *We'll cook gnocchi together at your place. L X*

She smiled and a warm cosy feeling pushed aside all her anxieties. *Food is not just for a hungry belly. It feeds the soul.* She hadn't understood what Maria had meant when she'd told her that but now she did. When you cooked with someone or for someone you loved then the love transferred to the food.

Leo wanted to cook with her. Leo wanted to stay the whole night with her. He wanted to be with her. The hope that had sprouted yesterday grew taller and, like the grapevine, tendrils curled around her heart, anchoring fast. Would he want to stay for ever because he wanted to?

She bit her lip again, this time tasting blood. During the early hours of the morning, with his masculine scent still on her sheets from the previous night, and with his tender voice in her head, she'd conjured up fairy tales of them together as a couple, together as parents of a black-haired, black-eyed baby and surrounded by the love of his family. A family so unlike her own, a family who adored children. The urge to ring him right then and blurt out the news had almost overpowered her.

But she'd held back. She wanted to do this the right way. She'd have the ultrasound first, check if the IUD was going to cause a problem and get all the facts before she spoke to him face to face. She had a plan and it was important to stick to it. The plan was the only thing she had.

She picked up the phone and dialled Mildura hospital's obstetric department. 'Hello, it's Abbie McFarlane, GP from Bandarra speaking. I need an urgent appointment with Alistair Macklin.'

Leo couldn't settle. He'd had the worst night's sleep in a long time, tossing and turning with snatches of dreams where Abbie lay in his arms one minute and had vanished in the next. He'd searched everywhere for her—running and calling, but he hadn't been able to find her. He'd woken with a start, his heart pounding and with a rushing return of the same unease he'd had when he'd first arrived back in Bandarra. He hadn't even realised he'd been living without it for the last few weeks until this morning.

He'd left home before the family were up and completed his rounds early. All his patients from yesterday were stable, which was great for them but left him with nothing much to do. He'd tossed a few balls to Alec, who'd now joined the Bandarra under-thirteens cricket team and was completely focused on improving his game. Then he'd gone for a long, hard bike ride with the Murray-to-Moyne crew. Hell, he'd even gone grocery shopping for tonight's dinner with Abbie, but nothing had completely banished the simmering sense of unease that bubbled inside him.

He checked his watch again. Abbie wasn't due to finish at the clinic for a few hours and he wasn't rostered on today but he had an increasing need to see her. He needed to breathe in her scent, lose himself in her clear rainforest-green eyes, wrap his arms around her and let her voice wash over him. Her voice, which could be soft and soothing one minute and deep and husky the next, and he couldn't get enough of it.

As he walked towards the clinic's front door, ominous black clouds gathered in the west. Leo frowned, his years in the city never completely removing the country's preoccupation with the weather. Bandarra always needed water but rain during harvest was never welcome. His hand turned the large door handle and he stepped inside the cool and welcoming clinic.

He was immediately struck by the quiet. The

front desk, or 'command centre' as Abbie jokingly called it, was empty and Jessica, the receptionist who kept command, was nowhere to be seen. No patients waited in the comfortable chairs and the toys that usually lay scattered were stacked neatly into a box. Had he got the roster wrong? He glanced at the movement board and saw Abbie was signed in and a zip of delight shot through him. As there were no patients, perhaps he could convince her to cut out early.

He walked down the corridor to her office and knocked on the door. After a moment's silence he pressed his ear to the door and, as he couldn't hear the murmuring of voices, he opened the door. 'Surprise.'

But the room was empty, although the computer purred away, so he decided to wait for Abbie and deal with his email on a big screen rather than his phone. With only a few days before he returned to Melbourne, his receptionist was firing emails to him every hour as she adeptly juggled his schedule between his rooms and Melbourne City.

'Abbie, Alistair Macklin's—oh, Leo.' Jessica stalled in the doorway, her hand on her watch.

'Sorry, I thought Abbie was here doing paper-work.'

He smiled at the flustered receptionist. 'I'm looking for her too so I thought I'd check my emails while I waited. Do you want me to give her the message?'

Jessica hesitated as if she was in two minds and then she rechecked her watch. 'Do you mind? It's just I was supposed to have left half an hour ago. Abbie can't be far away because she didn't sign out with me.' She slid a fax onto the desk. 'Just make sure she gets this message about Alistair Macklin changing the date and time. I've moved all her patients over to your clinic in the morning so she's got the whole day off.'

'Can do.' He grinned at Jess, who was usually so efficient and well organised. 'Does that mean I have to start at eight tomorrow?'

'Oh, yes, sorry.' The words floated on a wail. 'I know I should have asked you first but all of this happened so quickly and—'

The sound of an impatient horn beeped three times. 'And Gavin's waiting for you. It's fine, Jess, just go.'

'Thanks, Leo, I owe you one, but make sure you give Abbie the paper.'

He waved her out of the door. 'Consider it done.' He was glad to help out while he was here so Abbie could attend one of the professional development seminars at the Mildura Base hospital. As he picked up the paper to place it under his phone so he didn't forget about it, his gaze caught the word *Obstetric*. Was Abbie brushing up on her baby-catching skills? He looked more closely and read, *Obstetric Clinic, patient Abbie McFarlane #71892*.

His mouth dried as his throat constricted, and the paper crumpled in his hand.

Abbie was pregnant.

His hand jerked up to his head as dread skittered through him, screaming. Pregnant.

No way, not possible.

Somehow his brain managed to kick in, all rational and matter-of-fact. Abbie had an IUD and there'd only been that *one* time they hadn't used a condom. One time. Once. What were the odds?

But, despite the reassurances, his eyes stayed glued on the words *Obstetric Clinic*. It didn't say 'gynaecology', meaning an annual check-up and pap test; it said *Obstetrics*. That meant pregnancy.

A baby.

His blood pounded so hard and fast it roared in his ears. He heard Dom's voice, Christina's grief and his chest seized. *I hate you.* The past hauled him down, back to black and bleak days. He couldn't do this again. He dragged in a ragged breath, desperately trying to push away the voices.

A baby.

His baby.

An image of a plump, round-faced baby with curly hair and large round eyes rose in his mind and the panic eased slightly. *His* baby. For a second, an incredible feeling of warmth spread through him before the fear returned, along with Christina's bleak and miserable expression.

A clap of thunder broke overhead, making him jump. He turned towards the window as huge drops of rain pelted against the glass, quickly joining together to form wide rivulets of water. The rumble of more thunder sounded in the distance.

I don't want to have a child on my own. Abbie's words rumbled in his mind before striking him like lightning and burning into him. She'd been adamant she didn't want a child. He could clearly see the straight set of her shoulders and the legacy of Greg's treatment of her still hovering around her. He could hear her firm voice as she spoke about her miserable childhood, and her determination that no kid would go through what she'd been through.

Never dependent on anyone ever again. His breathing sped up, coming in hard and fast runs, and he was barely able to force air down into his tight chest. There could only be *one* reason for this appointment. Only one reason for the urgency and reorganisation of the clinic and patients.

He dry retched. The thought of a baby terrified him, the thought of even trying to have a future with Abbie scared him rigid, but the realisation of what Abbie planned to do completely gutted him.

Abbie walked through the door. 'Oh, hello. Isn't the rain wonderful?'

Leo dragged his gaze upwards, his knuckles white, still clutching the paper. Her trademark glossy caramel curls framed her face as usual but he caught the vestiges of strain in the creases around her generous mouth. 'Not for the grapes.'

Her brow creased slightly. 'Oh, right, I didn't think about that. Still, you're a lovely surprise.'

She sounded distracted and rounded the desk, putting her arms around his neck, kissing him lightly. Almost absently. 'I didn't expect to see you until dinner.'

Leo's brain struggled to function. Part of him wanted to haul her against him and kiss her hard and part of him didn't want to touch her. Somewhere in the 'common sense' zone of his mind he knew he should just let things play out as they would have done if he hadn't come into the office. But the reverberating words 'Obstetric Clinic' boomed in his head, driving out every coherent thought.

'Are you pregnant?'

Leo's black eyes glittered with anger as his scorching and accusatory words burned into her. Memories of Greg stormed in and she started to shake. *How do you know?* Her breath picked up, fast and shallow. This wasn't how she'd planned to tell him. Not like this, when she could hear and see his acrimony. See the terrors of his past so clearly on his face. She bit her lip and faced him down. 'What sort of question is that?'

'One that deserves an answer.' He shoved a piece of paper at her, his hand rigid with a vibrating fury that clung to every part of him.

A flash of lightning lit up the room and with trembling hands she saw the familiar logo of the Mildura Base hospital, read her name and the details of her appointment at the obstetric clinic. A jet of self-righteous resentment surged through her. 'This is private. How did you get this?'

He met her glare with one of his own, completely devoid of any contrition. 'Jess had to leave and I took the message. But that's irrelevant.' He shot out of his chair and towered over her. 'Why didn't you tell me?'

The oxygen in the air vanished, immediately replaced by fear. *Because of this reaction.* 'It's my problem.'

Leo roared. 'It's a baby.'

The deafening sound of the rain on the tin roof seemed to amplify his anger. She shuddered at his rage, pushing down the memories that threatened to swamp her and forcing herself to stand firm. 'I know it's a baby.' *Against all odds, it's the gift of a baby.* 'A baby who, given the fact I have an IUD, shouldn't even exist but does.'

'*Dio mio*, so your solution is a termination?' He slammed his fist into his palm, his eyes wild and his gaze filled with disgust.

Her stomach dropped to the floor, nausea

swamping her, and she gripped the edge of the desk as her head spun. Her chest burned at his betrayal, turning four glorious weeks into bitter dust. 'That's what you think I'd do?'

His arms flew into the air, gesticulating passionately. 'Your secrecy, the urgency of the appointment; what else was I to think?' But for the first time a hint of uncertainty ringed him.

Cloaking sadness made her gag and she dragged in a breath. 'You really don't know me at all, do you.'

'Of course I don't. We only met a month ago.'

His words knocked all the air out of her lungs, leaving nothing but aching cramp.

His defiant stance matched his words. 'You told me you didn't want to have children.'

'And, just like that, you tried and judged me.' She crossed her arms over her chest, trying to stop herself from shaking. 'Leo, I know this is a shock. I'm still reeling too but listen to me. I'm seeing Alistair to have a scan. The IUD could cause problems and I wanted to have all the information first-hand so you and I could discuss it.' A sigh shuddered out of her. 'So we know exactly what we're dealing with.'

'We're dealing with our baby.'

She nodded in silence. At least they agreed on that much. For a moment his face softened and she thought he'd extend his arms out towards her like he did so often, and then pull her gently against his chest before burying his face in her hair and whispering, *tesoro*. But he didn't.

'Right.' He dragged a hand through his hair and started to pace, the surgeon-in-charge. 'And if everything's fine then you'll come to Melbourne.'

She started and hope spluttered. 'You *want me* to come to Melbourne with you?'

He rubbed the scar on his chin. 'It's not really a choice now, is it?'

Resignation and anger simmered through his stark words, hurling hurt at her. Abbie braced herself. 'We have a choice, Leo; I'm not like Christina, I'm not an unskilled eighteen-year-old from a tiny town in rural Italy.'

He stiffened and spoke through tight lips. 'But you're pregnant with my child so we have to do what's right by the child.'

She'd expected this and her legs trembled and she locked her knees. 'And what's that?'

'We give it a go.'

She stared into his eyes, trying to read them,

but got nothing. *Give it a go.* What was that code for? 'Give what a go?'

'Us.' His mouth flattened into a resentful line full of past hurt. 'You never know; this time the odds might fall my way.'

Might. Her heart thundered hard against her chest, each beat excruciatingly painful as he seemingly ignored all the wonderful moments they'd shared in the last few weeks. 'And if it doesn't work out, what then?'

He frowned. 'Abbie, we've only known each other a month. You understand what that means? Believe me, I know that's not long enough to predict anything.'

You understand. Like rose thorns tearing through skin, his words ripped through her. The same words her father had used against her. The same words Greg had flung at her. *He doesn't love you.* The agony of that realisation bore down on her so hard she could feel herself crumpling under the weight.

He didn't love her. Just like he hadn't loved Christina. His sense of put-upon duty would eventually make their life a misery. Just like with Greg. She refused to put a child in the middle of a toxic relationship where fear and uncertainty ruled their lives. Warrior Abbie stormed to the languishing box that had been opened for a month, dusted it off and oiled the hinges. Abbie knew exactly what she had to do.

Leo's gut cramped as Abbie's face suddenly hardened and images of Christina and Dom crashed in on him. Two people he'd let down so badly. 'Hell, Abbie, I'm trying to be adult about this.'

Abbie's hands clenched. 'What I understand is that you think you have to "do the right thing" but you really don't want to.'

'Come on, Abbie. Be fair. This was a fling. Neither of us expected this to go beyond next week.'

'So it's all about the brevity of our time together and not the substance?' She crossed her arms tightly. 'I'm not Christina, Leo. We laugh together, we share common interests but you've reduced all that to long odds.'

Living with you is worse than hell. Leo dragged his hand across the back of his neck, trying to think when he really wanted to run. 'Look, I'm willing to give it a good shot.'

'A good shot?' Her voice rose, the tone sheer incredulity. 'But if it doesn't work you can just leave any time. Thanks for the vote of confidence in us; that's a really committed start.'

Her words bit but he had right on his side. 'Look, I once stood in a church and promised to love a woman I barely knew and I let her down badly. I'm not doing that again.'

Her face blanched and she spoke flatly. 'I'm not asking for marriage, Leo.'

Shock ricocheted through him and his heart stumbled on the unspoken request in her soft voice. A request he couldn't honour. *She loves you.* Abbie loved him and wanted his love in return. *Dio mio*; he couldn't give her that.

His jaw ached. 'I'm sorry, Abbie, but I can't promise you anything because life isn't like that.' *I can't promise anyone anything because I just let them down.*

'Because you might fail?' Blazing green eyes speared him, pinning him against an invisible wall. 'So you won't even really start? You just told me you were being an *adult*.'

Exasperation whipped him. 'Of course I'm starting. We need to live together to see if it can work.'

'You already have us failed because of what happened with Christina. I think you're letting the teenage "you" make really bad decisions about your life now.' She stepped away from him and around the desk, putting distance and an obstacle between them.

He ignored the ripple of anxiety that crept through him. 'You have no idea what you're talking about.'

She shook her head. 'No, that's where you're wrong. You married Christina because she connected you with Dom. But guilt, grief and misguided duty are not the foundations for a marriage. Is it any wonder it didn't work?'

Her words pounded him with the truth, harsh and real, and he held on to his control by a thread, trying not to yell at her, hating her expression when he did. 'And we probably won't work either but there's a baby so we should at least try.'

'Well, at least you've openly said it.' Pity swirled in her eyes and sat firmly on her cheeks. 'There's no point then, is there? I will not be the victim of your over-developed sense of duty that will eventually destroy us.'

Her hands spread out in front of her in entreaty. 'I'm sorry that your brother died but it wasn't your fault. It was appalling timing following an argument but it could have happened to anyone.

Unfortunately, it happened to Dom. Now you've embedded blame into your heart, not just for his death but for Christina's depression as well and it's stopping you from living your life.'

He wanted to put his hands over his ears but instead he heard himself yelling, 'I'm a rich and successful surgeon.'

Abbie didn't flinch at his bluster. All he could see on her face was sorrow. Sorrow for him.

'It's not a fulfilled life, though, is it?'

Her quiet words lashed him with their honesty and he fought back, wanting to hurt her. 'This from a woman whose approach to life was to lock herself away and deny herself any pleasure. At least I'm out there and not hiding.'

This time she flinched and her voice trembled. 'Against every part of my better judgement, I gave in to pure hedonism with you, did things your way, and I can't see it making either of us very happy right now.'

She spun away, wrapping her arms tightly around her before turning back. She breathed out a long, slow breath. When she opened her eyes, compassion and affection stood side by side, edged with grief. 'I love you, Leo, but I can't compete with your guilt because it's eating away at you and holding you apart from everyone who loves you.'

He didn't want to hear her telling him she loved him. He didn't want to hear anything more about himself so he rolled his eyes, needing to deflect her words. 'Here we go, more navel-gazing pop-psychology. I'm sorry I don't love you, Abbie, but let's get real, we only agreed to sex.' He ignored the appalled and horrified charmer deep within who always kept him civil.

A flicker of something he couldn't name raced across her face before she spoke slowly and clearly, her words devoid of all emotion. 'You used me and work to try and forget and I let you.'

For a nanosecond, every part of him stilled. Then bile scalded his throat, his chest burned so tight he couldn't breathe and every muscle in his body tensed, ready to run. She saw right through him. Saw his fears, saw clear down to his bruised and battered soul and it terrified him. No one had ever got that close before. No one.

He brushed all her words aside with the sweep of his hand. 'None of this is relevant to the baby and that's what we're supposed to be talking about.'

Utter sadness lined her face. 'You really don't get it, do you?'

His hand tugged at his hair. 'I get I'm going to be a father and, with my workload, both of you need to be with me in Melbourne.'

She nailed him with a flinty glare. 'Go back to Melbourne so you can bury yourself in work and see the baby when it fits in with your schedule?' The scoff was bitter and anger laced every word. 'You can get a nanny for that, Leo, and I reject your offer. I deserve better than that. Our baby deserves better than that and if you can't love us then we're not going to sit on the sidelines, biding our time while you pretend to try and then leave us anyway. I won't live under that threat.'

He couldn't fathom her thinking. 'It's a plan, not a threat!'

'It's a threat.'

Abbie turned towards the door and something inside him tore apart but he couldn't give in to that pain. Instead, he fought for the child. 'How can you walk away from a chance to give this baby the family it deserves?'

She twirled back, a mixture of love and contempt swirling in her eyes. 'I'm staying in Bandarra and this baby will be surrounded by family, Leo. Your family. The one you choose to hide from most of the time.' She pushed her hair out of her eyes, the action decisive. 'I'll get Alistair to send a copy of the ultrasound to you. Goodbye, Leo.'

Resentment poured through him. 'You can't just walk out in the middle of this; we haven't made any decisions.'

'I've made mine.' She stepped through the doorway and disappeared from sight.

CHAPTER ELEVEN

ABBIE stared at the rain. The heavy and cascading type of rain usually found in tropical far north Queensland, not outback New South Wales. Rain that hadn't eased in three days. The town's initial delight at the much-needed water had turned to unease and foreboding. Flood warnings had been issued and the SES had launched into action, sandbagging the river to protect the town. Not since 1970 had the town been faced with a peaking river that threatened to break its banks and spread its damage far and wide.

Low-lying orchards, still struggling to recover from the shocking heat two years ago, now lay flooded with their crops unable to be harvested. The wine industry faced a shortage of grapes to turn into premium wine and the farmers had taken another hit, lurching from drought to flood within seventy-two hours.

Abbie tried to care. Her town, her house, the hospital, her patients' livelihoods—all were under threat and she'd been busy going through the motions of preparing for the flood but, as she packed up equipment and backed up computers, her thoughts were centred elsewhere. On the baby. On Leo. Her hand brushed her lower abdomen. *New life.*

Yesterday, Alistair Macklin had successfully removed her IUD and reassured her that, as it was so early in the pregnancy, the risk of a miscarriage was no greater than with any other pregnancy. The fact that this embryo had successfully embedded in the first place made her think it was very determined and unlikely to change its mind.

Determined like its father.

She blinked back the tears that had moved in the moment she'd walked out on Leo and now hovered permanently. Walking away had been the hardest thing she'd ever done in her life, but where was the choice? Had he loved her, things could have been different. Could have been wonderful. But the appalled look on his face when she'd told him she loved him had left her in no doubt. That and his duty-bound idea of 'giving it a good shot', which only meant delayed heartbreak because his heart wasn't in it. His resentment would turn into anger and she and the baby would endure the fallout.

As desperately hard as it was, she wouldn't stay with a man who didn't love her. She'd fought for her right to be loved and she'd lost. No way was she ever going to beg for love. She had a child to raise and she had to be strong for that child. The one-month fling was over and an affair was all it had meant to Leo. Life moved on and somehow she had to as well.

But knowing all that didn't stop her heart from bleeding. Bleeding for Leo. He'd accused her of hiding from life and yet he was doing exactly the same thing, only in a different way. Her phone rang, interrupting her unwanted thoughts. 'Abbie McFarlane.'

'Abbie, it's Jackie Casterton, from Riverflats.' The experienced mother's voice sounded extremely anxious. 'Hugh's got a really high fever and extreme pain in his left ear. I wanted to bring him in to you but my car won't start.'

Doctor Abbie immediately surfaced through the quagmire of Abbie's personal life, happy to have something concrete to concentrate on. 'No problem, Jackie. The clinic's really quiet due to the rain and my four-wheel drive will go anywhere. How's the road out to your place?'

'It's still open.'

'Great. I'll bring the medication with me to make things easier all round.'

'Oh, Abbie, thank you so much. Honk when you get to the gate.'

'Will do.' She rang off, picked up her bag and walked out to see Jess. 'Murphy and I are going to the Castertons'. I'll be in range so call me if there's anything urgent; otherwise I'll be back in an hour.'

Jess nodded. 'If anything comes up I can always ring Leo. He's in town until Saturday, right?'

Abbie forced herself to sound normal. 'That's my understanding.' Not wanting to further the conversation, she grabbed her Driza-bone jacket off the coat-stand and walked out into the rain.

Leo stared at the image on his phone for the trillionth time in twenty-four hours. Yesterday he'd worked a full day in the clinic, burying himself in work so he had no time to think of anything other than a myriad of signs, symptoms and diagnoses. It hadn't really worked. His blazing outrage at

Abbie for not only walking out on him but disregarding his plan for them still burned hot.

He should be relieved she didn't want to move in with him. Be relieved that she'd rejected his honour-generated offer that had terrified him and thrown up images of his marriage. But there'd been no relief to the crushing maelstrom of emotions that simmered inside him.

Abbie of all people should know that a child needed both parents around.

He re-read the text that had come from Alistair Macklin with the ultrasound picture. *All looks fine.* He gazed at the peanut-shaped blob that was his offspring and gave thanks because nothing else in his life was fine. Everything else pretty much sucked.

'Leo, come!' Stefano hailed him from the winery door.

Leo pocketed his phone and strode towards his father as they made their way down to the vines. Muddy water eddied around their feet as they headed towards the other workers sandbagging the levee and shoring up what they could against the likelihood of a flood. Fortunately, all the buildings of the winery were on higher ground but many of the vines grew on the fertile flood plains of a river than hadn't flooded in decades.

Leo glanced at the clusters of dark purple grapes. 'What's the chance of Downey mildew?'

Stefano grimaced. 'If we get the usual March heat after this rain, the Petit Verdot are at risk.' His boots slurped in the mud. 'That's if the vineyard doesn't flood and we lose the vines as well.'

Leo hated seeing his father's life's work at risk from omnipotent weather. 'At least you've harvested the whites.'

'True. We give thanks for that.' He sighed and clapped his hand on Leo's shoulder. 'But we've weathered worse than this, your *mamma* and me. Vines can be replanted but lives cannot.'

Leo stiffened as still shots of memory flashed in sequence—the terrifying crack of the falling tree branch, Christina's screams, the image of his brother disappearing—all reverberating through him. Whether it was the touch of his father's hand or the fact that Stefano had mentioned Dom or even the mess of the last few days, but long-unspoken words rushed out. 'I still miss him.'

Stefano nodded, his face lined with understanding. '*Figlio mio*, we all do. Your *nonna* visits the billabong, your *mamma* lights candles, and my love for him goes into every bottle of wine I make. But you—I worry for you.'

His chest constricted. 'No one needs to worry about me.' The staccato ring of his words couldn't block Abbie's voice that rang loud in his head. *You've embedded blame into your heart...and it's stopping you from living your life.*

'You've stayed away too long. You need to come home more often and use your family to find a way to feel closer to Dom.' Stefano placed his fist against his heart. 'There is no fault, Leo, just sadness. Let go of the regret. It's time to honour your brother by being at peace with yourself.'

Peace. Leo didn't know what the hell that was or how to even start to find it. His father had never spoken this directly to him but, try as he might, he couldn't find the words to explain the chaos in his heart. Instead, he ramped up the pace of his shovelling, blocking out the current mess that was his life. As the rain trickled down his back, it sparked the memory of the silky touch of Abbie's hair against his skin, and the scent of it flared in his nostrils. A sensation rolled through him, trickling down into the dark places that usually remained untouched. Was that peace?

I reject your offer.

The sensation vanished and he gritted his teeth. He and his father worked in silence, both busy with their own thoughts. Time ticked by and it was Stefano who finally broke the quiet.

'I think this time coming home isn't all bad, eh? I see you took my advice.' Stefano shovelled sand into hessian bags and gave a deep belly laugh at Leo's blank expression. 'I know; it surprised me and your *mamma* too. Abbie McFarlane.'

A prickle of apprehension ran through him. 'What about her?'

Stefano winked. 'She's a real woman with heart and soul. Not like Christina who you thought would fill the gap your brother had left. Not like the plastic types you've chased since. Now, Abbie McFarlane is a woman who could make you happy.'

I reject your offer. Leo grunted as bitterness boiled inside him. 'Really, Papà? Well, she doesn't think I can make her happy.'

His father frowned at his tone. 'I'm sorry. I saw the love on her face for you and I thought she'd accept your proposal.'

Leo hefted another bag onto the levee. 'I didn't

propose. I asked her to come to Melbourne and live with me.'

'Ah!' The sound said it all. 'Leo, women want marriage, commitment and the promise of babies.'

The pent-up emotions of the last two days poured out of him as the wind whipped him. 'You think I don't know that? I've had one nightmare marriage and that's why I've avoided serious relationships for years.' He ran his hand through his rain-drenched hair. 'Both Abbie and I agreed that neither of us wanted marriage or babies, which is why it was a perfect holiday thing.'

Stefano leaned on his shovel, confusion and concern clear on his face. 'If it was just sex, why did you ask her to go back with you to Melbourne?'

Just sex. Indignation swooped through Leo, irritating and shocking him in equal parts. He opened his mouth to object to his father's statement, to say it was more than just sex, but different words tumbled out instead. Words he hadn't spoken to anyone. 'Because she's pregnant.'

Stefano sat down hard on the bags. *'Dio mio. A baby?'*

He shook his head and muttered what sounded

like, 'Doctors should know better.' Censure rode on his face and threaded through his words. 'She's pregnant with your child and you ask her to live with you? I thought I'd raised you to do the honourable thing. Now I understand why she refused your tawdry offer.'

Leo threw up his hands, regretting his disclosure. 'She doesn't want marriage, Papà. That isn't the issue.'

'What does she want?'

'Something I can't give her.'

His father's dark eyes glinted harshly. 'Do you love her?'

Leo's gaze slid away. 'I've known her a month! Hell, I knew Christina for longer and look how that ended up.'

'Time is irrelevant and that's not what I asked. Do you love her?'

Leo filled another bag. 'I admire her.'

'Admire her?' His father trembled with anger but he didn't roar. His controlled voice was ten times worse. 'This from the man who's been in her bed for weeks?'

'Don't censure me on this, Papà. We're two consenting, mature adults who knew what we were doing.'

'Obviously.' Stefano's hands rose high in the air. 'And now there is a child. A Costa! Family.'

Leo matched his father's glare. 'And I'm willing to give it a good shot to see if I can make something that was never planned work, but she refuses.'

'You told Abbie this? Can you hear yourself?'

I can't promise you anything. His own bald words deafened him and he fought against them. 'I offered her the opportunity to try. What's love, anyway, but an overrated word?'

'If that's what you believe, then I have let you down badly.' A sigh shuddered through Stefano. 'For years I've accepted you are a man and I've let you make your own way, hoping you would learn, but you've stayed away, replaced real connections with superficial ones and locked the family and love out of your life. It is lonely, *sì?*'

Leo wanted to scream, *No*, but he heard Abbie's voice echoing in his head. *Your guilt...it's holding you apart from everyone who loves you.*

His father pressed on. 'So I tell you now what I should have told you years ago. Loving someone isn't comfortable or easy, but she's the last person you think of when you fall asleep, the first person you think of when you wake up, and she's the person you want to share your day with, good or bad. She's the woman who annoys you to the point where you don't know if you want to yell at her or kiss her until the earth moves.'

Images and voices hammered him. Abbie in his arms, the intellectual arguments, the passionate sex and the snatches of contentment he'd never known before. Was that love?

Stefano fixed Leo with a look filled with the wisdom of life's hard lessons. 'But, most importantly, love is the woman who doesn't tell you what you want to hear but what you need to hear. With a woman like that by your side, then you know you are truly loved.'

You used me and work to try and forget.

It's not a fulfilled life, though, is it?

He broke out in a sweat. From the moment they'd met, Abbie hadn't let him get away with anything. She'd seen through every excuse and challenged him on everything he believed about himself. And she'd been right. He'd been hiding behind an accomplished career, believing that gave him a fulfilled life. But it gave him half a life and the rest was a thin veneer of perceived success that covered a giant empty cavern.

It had taken coming home and meeting her to finally face the truth. He needed her.

I love her. Oh, God, he loved her. What sort of fool was he that he'd loved a woman for weeks and had no clue?

And he'd thrown her precious love for him back at her in the worst way possible.

I deserve better than that. I won't live under that threat.

His heart broke open. Abbie, with her tilted chin, her caramel curls and her generous heart had stood her ground against his fears and her own and yet at the same time had tried valiantly to fight for him. For his messed-up, damaged heart.

And he hadn't fought for her.

He'd acted just like the bastards who'd passed through her life, taking what he wanted from her and then pushing her away with his half-baked attempt at duty. The words, 'give it a good shot' rang in his head. His gut clenched. No wonder she'd walked out on him. He'd forced her to go, pushing away the best thing that had ever happened to him.

The love of his life.

He ran his hands through his hair, the past

still holding him hostage. 'What if I stuff it up again?'

His father gave him a cryptic smile. 'Adults take risks, Leo. Make peace with yourself and open yourself up to the love of a good woman.'

'If she'll have me.'

Stefano nodded. 'That I can't answer. All I can say is—go now and build bridges to her heart.'

Leo didn't have to be told twice.

'What do you think, Murph?' Abbie had the windscreen wipers on full pelt and even then she could hardly see through the rain. 'This is our only choice now Old Man Creek's flooded.' She was on her way back from the Castertons, having started Hugh on antibiotics for a perforated eardrum. Poor kid; he'd been in a lot of pain. 'I guess we just keep going, taking it slowly.'

She changed into low gear, giving thanks she had the full tread of four-wheel drive wheels giving her traction against the slippery gravel that resembled a river of red mud more than a road. She wished she was home. Or already back at the clinic. It wasn't just that the road conditions were treacherous but, given a choice, she wouldn't be on this road today because it put her within five hundred metres of the Costas' front gate and even closer to the vines. No way was she ready to face Leo. Not yet. She needed to be completely on top of things next time they met—emotionally strong—and right now she was a very long way from that.

Most of her hoped he'd return to Melbourne and that it would be weeks before they had to talk again to sort out money and access. The whole situation had a surreal feel to it and she was happy to delay any decisions as long as possible. Delay everything until she'd worked out how to stop loving the father of her child. A child that would bind them together for ever. The irony that the baby now connected her with a family she couldn't be part of wasn't lost on her—their loyalties would lie with Leo. Did life have to be this hard?

The old wooden single-lane bridge came into view and, although the river ran high and fast, the bridge was still above the water line. 'We just need to get across the bridge and then we're on bitumen.'

Murphy barked his approval. Abbie knew how he felt. She wasn't keen on this bridge, even in good weather. Its narrowness and low sides always made her edgy. She hauled on the hand-brake and wound down her window, leaning out of the vehicle to double-check there wasn't a car coming in the opposite direction. Across the river she could vaguely make out the silhouette of men—Costa employees—building a levee bank to protect the vines. Her heart tore as her eyes disregarded her instructions and scanned the group for height—Leo stood out in any group. But the rain obscured details and she couldn't see much at all. She dragged her gaze to the other side of the bridge.

No cars.

Leaving her window open so she could see the side of the bridge, she slowly pressed the accelerator down. Rain drove into the cabin but it was better to be wet than misjudge things and end up over the side. Halfway over, she glanced up into the white glare of headlights. A car had pulled up and was waiting for her to cross. The lights dimmed and her mouth dried as an unmistakably tall man emerged from the car. Leo.

Her hand froze on the gear-stick and every part of her wanted to throw the truck into reverse and retreat but that wasn't possible. Even in dry conditions she wouldn't trust herself to manoeuvre a vehicle this size backwards over such a narrow bridge. Her heart hammered as she ran limited options through her head. She could just drive past him when she reached the other side but that would only antagonise him more. She knew he'd been bitterly furious at her for walking out on him and she didn't want to add to that. Somehow they had to find a way through this nightmare so they could be civil for the baby's sake.

Oh, dear God, but she wasn't quite ready to start now. She maintained her slow speed, purposely delaying the moment she'd have to greet him, knowing her heart would die just a little bit more when she spoke the words, *Hello, Leo.*

Between the pounding of the rain on the roof and the engine noise, nothing much else could be heard, although Abbie thought she heard a low drawn-out groan. It had probably come from her own lips as she crept inexorably closer to Leo and another difficult conversation.

The groan grew deeper and louder and then an almighty roar of splitting timber erupted around her and, before she could do a thing, the four-wheel drive rolled. Deafening noise bellowed as water rushed at her through the open window, filling her nose, her eyes and her mouth. Everything was black. Dazed and disoriented, she had no idea if she was up or down. *Get out!* All she knew was that if she stayed strapped in her seat she would die.

Fear both paralysed and galvanized her. Numb fingers pried at the seat belt as Murphy fell against her. The weight of the dog pinned her to the seat and, with an almighty heave, she pushed Murphy out of the window against the tide of water.

She gasped for air as she felt the seat belt come away and she tried to move through the open window but the pressure of the water pushed her back. She could see grey sky and kept her eyes glued to that as she tried again to move. To get out. To live. Suddenly she was flung sideways and the ripping noise of crumpling metal filled her ears.

Water covered her. She pushed upwards and broke the surface, coughing violently. Air. Sweet air. Her chest burned. *Get out, get out, get out.* She pulled up again, forcing her body out through the window. Red-hot pain seared her but her legs stayed put. Trapped.

Panic sucked at her and she fought against it as muddy water swirled up around her neck. Holding on to the car, she tilted her chin and sucked in air.

Air for herself, air for the baby. Twisting around, she tried again to free herself but she was pinned tight by the steering wheel and the dashboard. She breathed again. Water ran down her throat.

Coughing, she pushed her head back as far as she could and managed a breath. Darkness ate at the edges of her mind. Was this what her life had come to? First denied the man she loved and now the chance to raise his child.

No. She craned her head, trying to gain vital yet almost infinitesimal height to keep the water away from her nose. She heard Murphy's bark, the faint yell of voices. Help was coming. *Just keep going.* Her hands cramped, her fingers weakened, her legs screamed and every muscle burned as her body strained to stay above the water.

Then fire turned to ice and chilling pain dragged at her as she battled the morbid darkness that crushed her chest. Her energy drained away, completely consumed in the fight to escape, in the immense effort to breathe. A bright white light illuminated the darkness, promising blessed relief.

CHAPTER TWELVE

'NOOOOOOOOOO.' Leo's scream rent the air, slicing through the rain as the old timber bridge collapsed without warning, torn aside by the raging river as if it was as feeble as a matchstick model.

Build a bridge to her heart.

But the bridge had gone, taking Abbie with it, her four-wheel drive impotent against the surging flood waters that tossed it onto its roof and swept it downstream.

Move! He acted on instinct, driven forward by adrenaline and abject terror. He ripped back the tarp on the Ute and grabbed rope and then ran along the riverbank, through mud, through marsh, his eyes never moving from the four-wheel drive, which was being tossed around like a crisp packet. Did everyone he loved drown? Had he finally realised he loved Abbie, only to lose her? The thought struck him so hard he almost stopped breathing.

He saw a black and white flash and then Murphy appeared above water, valiantly swimming across the current. Hope burst through him. If the dog had got out then Abbie could too. *Let her live. Please, God, let her live.* His eyes strained through the rain, desperately searching for Abbie. For caramel hair. For a tilted and determined chin.

Nothing.

The levee bank builders, including his father, hearing the bridge collapse had rushed to the bank, their expressions frozen with shock.

The noise of crushing metal boomed around them. The vehicle slammed against a fallen red gum, its trajectory momentarily stopped as it became trapped between the tree and the bank.

Thank God. 'Call 000,' Leo yelled to the men. Lassoing a rope around his waist, he tied it firmly so it couldn't slide off. Floodwater currents could sweep a man away in a heartbeat so the rope was his only option.

He handed the other end of the tie to his father, forcing out the words against a constricted throat. 'It's Abbie.'

His father's dark eyes glowed with fear and memories. 'Go. Be careful.' His gloved hands gripped the rope as the other men gathered to help.

Leo waded into the water. Images of diving under murky water, images of Dom spurred him on. Water pulled at him, pushed him, eddying around him like a whirlpool, trying to suck him down into its muddy depths and keep him away from the driver's side of the truck. Vital seconds ticked past.

You can do this. He heard the voice of his brother, silent to him for so many years. *She's got a chance.*

'Abbie, I'm coming.' The wind caught his bellow and he struck out across the current.

The first sight he saw was her hair floating around her head like a halo. Her body was half out of the car and her face was underwater.

Dread sent its icy-cold fingers through him, squeezing his heart so tightly he thought it would cease beating. 'Abbie!' He heard his disembodied wail as he tried to lift her head well clear of the water. Her eyes had rolled back. His fingers fought to find her carotid pulse.

A flutter of a beat. Faint. Weak.

He had to get her out. With his arms around her chest, he gave an almighty pull, but her body refused to yield. *No!* Memories choked him and he tried again, refusing to give up another person he loved to this bloody river.

The water lashed them against the car, threatening to swamp Abbie again. He rechecked her pulse.

Barely there.

He struggled to hold her head above the water. How the hell could he hold her clear and give her mouth-to-mouth at the same time? He was losing her.

You can do this, Leo.

How? *Think.* He yelled to the men on the bank. 'She's trapped; get me an irrigation pipe.'

'We're getting it.' Voices relayed the message.

Water flowed across her chin. He needed the pipe now. Two minutes ago.

Was she breathing? He couldn't see her chest under the murky water. Had he got this close, only to lose her?

Anguish and terror tore through him.

'Abbie! I love you.' He shook her flaccid body. 'Come back to me. Don't ever leave me.'

I love you. The bright light that had promised Abbie relief from pain faded and she was plunged back into inky darkness and burning pain. Her chest screamed as her diaphragm moved up. Air hit her wet and aching lungs. She gasped, then gagged, vomiting into the river.

'Breathe, *tesoro*, breathe. Please just keep breathing.'

She breathed. She didn't have the energy to do anything else. Leo held her. Leo tilted her chin just above the water line; Leo's ragged voice surrounded her, soothing her as she battled the horrifying fear that she'd slip back under to that dark, dark place.

Leo. Her next breath came more easily.

'Abbie.' Leo's hand patted her on the cheek but she couldn't focus on him. She could only focus on her next breath. 'Abbie, the water is too high and you need to breathe through this pipe. Stefano's going to hold you and talk to you and I'm going to try and free your legs. Keep breathing, sweetheart; that's all you have to do. I'll do the rest.'

She felt the pipe against her lips and then another pair of arms wrapped around her.

'Like a snorkel, *sì*? Think of tropical fish. We're right here. Breathe in, breathe out.' Stefano's work-strong arms held her tightly. 'Leo's diving under.'

A moment later Leo's hands touched her on her body, trailing down her legs. Then the touch vanished.

'Abbie.' She heard the surgeon speaking to her, the tone almost vanquishing all traces of the petrified man. 'I have to break your leg to get you out.'

I don't care—just get me out. She couldn't speak and she had no energy to move but somehow she managed a nod.

'Bite the tube against the pain but don't scream. Just breathe through the pipe.'

She closed her mind to everything except the breath and then her body twisted violently and searing pain tore through her leg. Strong arms pulled her clear. The water receded to her chest and she let go of the tube. More arms hauled her up out of the water and dragged her over a log as excruciating pain the colour of fire—red, burnt orange and scorching yellow—tore through her.

Then she felt the soft mud of the bank against her back and rain on her face.

Safety. Blackness followed.

* * *

Abbie opened her eyes to flowers. Bright pink gerberas, purple lithianthus, fragrant white lilies, cheery yellow daisies and white roses. Three vases of white roses. She stared at them.

I love you. Had she imagined Leo saying that? Who knew what your brain did when it was being starved of oxygen?

She'd drifted in and out of consciousness and only had snatches of memory but she'd been certain Leo was with her when she'd been in the ambulance, gone into Theatre and been transferred to the ward.

He wasn't with her now.

'Hey, you're awake.' Anna put down her magazine. 'Are you hungry? I've got the chef on standby for whatever you want.'

Abbie gave her a wan smile, the idea of food curdling her stomach. 'I think a cup of tea with toast and Vegemite is all I really feel like.'

Anna stood up. 'Consider it done.' She squeezed her arm and walked out of the room as Stefano and Rosa walked in, bringing care and concern along with a large brown paper bag.

'My irrigation pipe has never been used as a snorkel before.' Stefano kissed her on both cheeks.

'Let's hope it never has to be again.' Abbie reached for his hand. 'Thank you for talking me through it.' She gave thanks she was alive but she really didn't want to think about how terrified she'd been so she changed the topic. 'How are the vines?'

'The rain has stopped and the levee bank is holding so we hold our breath for a few more days. Floods come and go, but it's the people we love who are important. You worry about yourself, OK?'

The people we love.

Rosa nodded in agreement. 'Maria sends her love and her bread. She's been in the kitchen since dawn, making you her special *zuppa* to make you strong again for the—'

Stefano's hand closed over Rosa's and she paused for half a beat before commenting on the flowers and greeting Chiara, who'd just arrived.

The baby. Leo had told them about the baby. The baby that may or may not still be alive after possible oxygen deprivation.

She let their conversation float around her, dutifully answered questions when asked and accepted Anna's tea and toast. Leo's family surrounded her with love and chatter but the one person she desperately needed to talk to wasn't here.

I love you. Perhaps it had been anoxia-induced imaginings after all.

She stared at her toes that peeked out of a bright white plaster cast. The staff had been checking her circulation all night and her foot was toasty warm. She didn't really have much pain from her leg but, then again, perhaps pain was relative after yesterday's experience.

'*Dio mio.*' Leo strode into the room in green theatre scrubs, clutching a chart in his broad strong hand. The quintessential surgeon in charge. 'What are you all doing here? Abbie needs rest.' His arm swept out towards the door. 'I don't know how you all got past Erin, but you have to go. Now.'

Stefano winked at Abbie and walked towards the door. Rosa stiffened and stalked towards the exit, giving her son a look that would reduce a lesser man to a gibbering mess and Chiara and Anna grumbled, telling Leo to never try using that tone at home, but they left anyway.

Silence crept into the room. A heavy, brooding silence that billowed into every corner, filled with a myriad of unresolved issues. Abbie bit her lip.

Leo finally spoke, throwing his hands up into the air. 'My family.'

'They mean well.'

He stood at the end of the bed, frowning and staring at her—a doctor attending to his patient. 'How are you?'

I don't know. She hated how they'd gone from such an easy camaraderie to this strained and torturous silence.

'Are you in pain?' He strode to the IV pump and checked the analgesia setting. 'I can boot it up.'

'No.' Her hand shot out and caught his arm. She needed to protect her baby and she needed a clear head to deal with Mr Costa, the surgeon. 'Leo, is the baby going to be OK?'

He stilled at her touch and it was like a knife slicing through her heart. She dropped her hand, certain that her near-death experience had tricked her mind into hearing words he hadn't spoken.

Leo ran his hand through his hair and it stood up in black spikes. 'I spoke with Alistair Macklin and he said, "Wait and see." You're fine so we have to assume that the baby got enough oxygen too.'

Panic fluttered through her. 'I was anoxic,

though. I saw the white light; I heard things I don't think were said.' She gripped the edge of the top sheet. 'We're doctors; we both know about the chemical changes in the brain just before death and I had that moment of euphoria which means I was oxygen starved.'

He kept staring at her, his eyes boring into hers, filled with swirling emotions that her fuzzy brain failed to decipher.

He dropped his gaze and wrung his hands. 'I heard Dom.'

'You heard your brother?' Confusion tugged at her. Why would he have heard voices? 'But you weren't drowning.'

He flinched. 'When I was in the river, I heard Dom's voice—as clear as if he was standing next to me—telling me you had a chance. It was like he was guiding me to you. I know it sounds crazy but I know it really happened.' He let out a long breath. 'So you can tell me because it can't be more out-there than that. What did you hear?'

What I wanted to hear.

'Abbie?' He sat down next to her, worry carved deeply around his eyes. 'Tell me.'

She swallowed and shook her head, not want-ing to see the same expression on his face she'd seen two days ago when he'd told her he didn't love her. 'It's not something you're going to want to hear.'

With a jerky movement, he picked up her hand. 'Abbie, you've always given it to me straight. It's part of what I love about you, so don't go all wussie on me now. Tell me.'

Her heart picked up as blood hammered loudly in her ears. 'You love me?'

He dropped his head forward, his broad shoulders shuddering before he lifted his gaze back to hers, his face drawn and haggard. 'I think I've loved you from the moment you told me in no uncertain terms it was up to Nonna to decide who her doctor was. It just took me until yesterday to realise.'

She wanted to throw herself into his love but she needed more. 'I had to almost drown before you knew you loved me?'

'No.' He clutched her hand with a desperate touch. 'I realised before that. I was on my way to tell you that you're my heart and soul when the bridge washed out. And I do love you, Abbie; you have to believe me. When I held you in my arms yesterday, so close to death, everything I'd valued about my life was reduced to worthless rubble.'

I love you. Don't ever leave me. Come back to me.

Joy exploded inside her, ricocheting through her and lighting up all the darkness. 'You called me back.' Her hand stroked his cheek. 'I'd given up, it was all too hard and then I heard your voice, telling me you loved me.'

'And I do.' His deep voice quivered with emotion. 'I love you with every part of me.'

He truly loved her. Her heart opened wide and she wrapped her arms around his neck.

Very carefully, he lay down next to her, gathering her close and burying his face in her hair. 'I'm so sorry I've been the biggest jerk on the planet. You were right. I'd been keeping everyone at arm's length for so long and it took your love to show me how wrong I'd been. I need you, Abbie.'

She held him tightly. 'I need you too.'

'With you, I've made peace with my past and now you and our baby are my future. Will you marry me?'

She stared at him, loving that he would offer her that, but not needing it. 'I know how you feel about marriage, Leo, and I told you, I don't need to get married. Your love is commitment enough.'

He shook his head, his expression as serious as she'd ever seen. 'No, it isn't. I want to stand up in front of my family and pledge my love for you. For our child. I want it on the public record that I will do everything and give my all to you, the love of my life. You deserve this and anything less isn't enough.'

His love surrounded her and she knew down to her soul she'd finally chosen a man who put her ahead of himself. A man who would stay with her, no matter what, but the need to test that lingered. 'So you'll love me even when I disagree with you?'

He kissed her hard. 'Especially when you disagree with me. I'll even try my best not to yell.'

She smiled at him. 'You're Italian; it's a given.' Resting her head on his shoulder, she gloried in the way his arms sheltered her. 'And you'll love me even though I'll never be able to wear clothes with your style and flair?'

He grinned. 'I'm Italian; it's a given.'

She laughed, embracing the sheer wonder

of being loved unconditionally. 'In that case, I accept.'

His answering kiss was all she needed.

EPILOGUE

THE launch of La Bella's Petit Verdot was in full swing. The press had declared it a 'sweet, spicy and appealing red with immense cellaring capabilities', which was sweet news indeed. It meant the wine could become a collector's item as it was one of only a handful of red wines produced two years ago due to the crop losses of the floods.

Family and friends gathered in the shady courtyard of the restaurant, gorging themselves on the bountiful amounts of food, all made from local produce. Abbie snuck more than one slice of her favourite *quattro formaggi* wood-fired pizza, justifying to herself that the calcium in cheese was important for healthy bones.

She wandered over to the courtyard gate and stepped into the garden. Murphy immediately trotted up to her followed by a bouncing and enthusiastic puppy that ran circles around him. Murphy gave her a look as if to say, "Do I really have to put up with this?"

Laughing, she patted both dogs. 'Hey, Alec, you got a border collie. Good choice.'

The teenager grinned. 'They're the best dogs, Abbie. Murph taught me that.'

She'd kept in contact with the boy and Murphy had stayed with him occasionally when Alec needed him or when Murphy had needed to escape the city. 'How's mum?'

'I'm great.' Penny scooped up the puppy and cuddled it.

Her face glowed with health and an air of contentment circled her. Unless someone took a close look and saw the faint scar of a tracheostomy, no one would know that she'd faced down death and won. She hooked a lead onto the puppy's bright red collar. 'Alec, if you want the top pick of Chiara's mingleberry jam you better come now because a tour bus just pulled in.'

With a wave they walked back inside. What had started out as a kitchen-table enterprise using the Cellar Door as an outlet had grown into a thriving business for Chiara that saw her products in delicatessens far away from Bandarra.

'Abbie.' A deep voice made her turn.

Stefano kissed her on both cheeks and handed her a glass of wine.

She tilted her glass toward him before she took a sip. 'It's a great party and a sensational wine.'

Her father-in-law smiled in his quiet way. 'My love for Dom and all my family is always there in my wine, but this one, I dedicate to you.'

'Really?' A bone-deep thrill rushed through her. 'I don't know what to say except, thank you.' The Costas had enveloped her into their family without a moment's hesitation and for that she loved them dearly. After years of not having family, she now had one in abundance.

'No, I'm thanking you. You brought Leo back to us.'

She shook her head. 'I think he was ready.'

Stefano put his hand on her shoulder, his expression serious. 'Never underestimate the power of love, Abbie.'

'Papà, are you philosophising again?'

They both turned and dark twinkling eyes winked at Abbie. Eyes filled with love and commitment. Eyes that made her knees go weak every time she saw them.

'*Nonno.*' A dark-eyed, curly-headed toddler leaned off Leo's shoulders, his arms outstretched toward his grandfather.

Leo reached up and lifted the child free. 'Papà, your grandson wants you.'

Stefano put out his arms to receive the child. 'Dante, let's go and look at the vines.'

'Grapes.' Dante extended a pudgy finger toward the vineyard.

'Smart boy.' His grandfather grinned as he strode toward his beloved vines.

Abbie waved to her son as he happily went with his beloved grandfather. Motherhood had exceeded all her dreams and she often had to pinch herself that this really was her life. Leo's arms circled her waist and he dropped his face into her hair. Love surrounded her and she leaned back into him, never tiring of his touch or the shelter of his arms. 'Where have you been hiding?'

'I took Dante and Nonna to the water-hole.'

She turned in his arms and smiled. For the last two years, Leo had accompanied his Nonna on her visits to the waterhole and whenever they visited Bandarra, which was about six times a year, he rode his bike out there. 'I'm glad. Dante loves it out there.'

Leo grinned. 'Well, he started life out there so perhaps he has a strong connection to the place like we do but for a different reason.' He wound a finger around one of her curls. 'The twins are busy earning money for a trip to Italy.'

Anna's daughters, at fourteen, were growing into beautiful and determined young women. 'Lauren was telling me all about an exchange program she wants to do next year.'

He nodded, trailing his finger down her cheek. 'The problem is they're underage so they can't work at the cellar door so they've started a baby-sitting club.'

His touch sent a tingle skating through her, a sensation that their time together had only height-ened. 'That sounds like a good idea.'

'I thought so. In fact, they suggested they mind Dante for an hour so we can enjoy ourselves.'

His finger barely touched her chin but every part of her hummed with anticipation. 'Enjoy our-selves at the party?'

His smile carved a dimple into his cheek and his eyes danced with wicked intent. 'They didn't specify *where* we enjoy ourselves. I was thinking more along the lines of the cottage.'

She rose up on her toes and put her arms around his neck, loving that his desire for her was as potent as the day they'd met. 'I love the way you think.'

'I love you.'

And of that she had no doubt.

MEDICAL™

Large Print

Titles for the next six months...

February

WISHING FOR A MIRACLE — Alison Roberts
THE MARRY-ME WISH — Alison Roberts
PRINCE CHARMING OF HARLEY STREET — Anne Fraser
THE HEART DOCTOR AND THE BABY — Lynne Marshall
THE SECRET DOCTOR — Joanna Neil
THE DOCTOR'S DOUBLE TROUBLE — Lucy Clark

March

DATING THE MILLIONAIRE DOCTOR — Marion Lennox
ALESSANDRO AND THE CHEERY NANNY — Amy Andrews
VALENTINO'S PREGNANCY BOMBSHELL — Amy Andrews
A KNIGHT FOR NURSE HART — Laura Iding
A NURSE TO TAME THE PLAYBOY — Maggie Kingsley
VILLAGE MIDWIFE, BLUSHING BRIDE — Gill Sanderson

April

BACHELOR OF THE BABY WARD — Meredith Webber
FAIRYTALE ON THE CHILDREN'S WARD — Meredith Webber
PLAYBOY UNDER THE MISTLETOE — Joanna Neil
OFFICER, SURGEON...GENTLEMAN! — Janice Lynn
MIDWIFE IN THE FAMILY WAY — Fiona McArthur
THEIR MARRIAGE MIRACLE — Sue MacKay

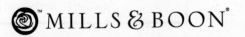

MILLS & BOON

0111 LP 2P P2 Medical

MEDICAL™

Large Print

May

DR ZINETTI'S SNOWKISSED BRIDE	Sarah Morgan
THE CHRISTMAS BABY BUMP	Lynne Marshall
CHRISTMAS IN BLUEBELL COVE	Abigail Gordon
THE VILLAGE NURSE'S HAPPY-EVER-AFTER	Abigail Gordon
THE MOST MAGICAL GIFT OF ALL	Fiona Lowe
CHRISTMAS MIRACLE: A FAMILY	Dianne Drake

June

ST PIRAN'S: THE WEDDING OF THE YEAR	Caroline Anderson
ST PIRAN'S: RESCUING PREGNANT CINDERELLA	Carol Marinelli
A CHRISTMAS KNIGHT	Kate Hardy
THE NURSE WHO SAVED CHRISTMAS	Janice Lynn
THE MIDWIFE'S CHRISTMAS MIRACLE	Jennifer Taylor
THE DOCTOR'S SOCIETY SWEETHEART	Lucy Clark

July

SHEIKH, CHILDREN'S DOCTOR...HUSBAND	Meredith Webber
SIX-WEEK MARRIAGE MIRACLE	Jessica Matthews
RESCUED BY THE DREAMY DOC	Amy Andrews
NAVY OFFICER TO FAMILY MAN	Emily Forbes
ST PIRAN'S: ITALIAN SURGEON, FORBIDDEN BRIDE	Margaret McDonagh
THE BABY WHO STOLE THE DOCTOR'S HEART	Dianne Drake

MEDICAL™

Large Print

May

DR ZINETTI'S SNOWKISSED BRIDE	Sarah Morgan
THE CHRISTMAS BABY BUMP	Lynne Marshall
CHRISTMAS IN BLUEBELL COVE	Abigail Gordon
THE VILLAGE NURSE'S HAPPY-EVER-AFTER	Abigail Gordon
THE MOST MAGICAL GIFT OF ALL	Fiona Lowe
CHRISTMAS MIRACLE: A FAMILY	Dianne Drake

June

ST PIRAN'S: THE WEDDING OF THE YEAR	Caroline Anderson
ST PIRAN'S: RESCUING PREGNANT CINDERELLA	Carol Marinelli
A CHRISTMAS KNIGHT	Kate Hardy
THE NURSE WHO SAVED CHRISTMAS	Janice Lynn
THE MIDWIFE'S CHRISTMAS MIRACLE	Jennifer Taylor
THE DOCTOR'S SOCIETY SWEETHEART	Lucy Clark

July

SHEIKH, CHILDREN'S DOCTOR...HUSBAND	Meredith Webber
SIX-WEEK MARRIAGE MIRACLE	Jessica Matthews
RESCUED BY THE DREAMY DOC	Amy Andrews
NAVY OFFICER TO FAMILY MAN	Emily Forbes
ST PIRAN'S: ITALIAN SURGEON, FORBIDDEN BRIDE	Margaret McDonagh
THE BABY WHO STOLE THE DOCTOR'S HEART	Dianne Drake

MILLS & BOON®

5|12|15